EMERALD DREAMS

*John & Bea ⟶ *!*

Forever Friends♡

EMERALD DREAMS

Sharon Graffius Kuhlman

S. Kuhlman (signature)

TATE PUBLISHING & *Enterprises*

This novel is a work of fiction. Names, descriptions, entities, and incidents included in the story are products of the author's imagination. Any resemblance to actual persons, events, and entities is entirely coincidental.

The opinions expressed by the author are not necessarily those of Tate Publishing, LLC.

Published by Tate Publishing & Enterprises, LLC
127 E. Trade Center Terrace | Mustang, Oklahoma 73064 USA
1.888.361.9473 | www.tatepublishing.com

Tate Publishing is committed to excellence in the publishing industry. The company reflects the philosophy established by the founders, based on Psalm 68:11,
"The Lord gave the word and great was the company of those who published it."

Book design copyright © 2010 by Tate Publishing, LLC. All rights reserved.
Cover design by Blake Brasor
Interior design by Stefanie Rane

Published in the United States of America

ISBN: 978-1-61739-066-1
1. Fiction, Historical
2. Ficiton, Coming of Age
10.09.22

DEDICATION

This book is dedicated to my husband, Tye, and son, Austin, the two greatest loves of my life.

Tye, your unwavering support has given me courage I did not know I had. Thank you for all the "special moments" that have added up to a wonderful life. My love for you has no boundaries.

And for my son, Austin, you are truly the light of my life! I fell in love with you the moment I set eyes on you. I can only hope as you venture out into this world that you remember to dream big and reach for the stars... it's all yours for the taking.

So, with that being said, this book is for "my boys." May I never forget to tell you how much I love you each and every day.

Many thanks to: Matthew, Jackson, Shelby (my number one fan), Alexandra and Abby. Friends: Barb Kuntz, Teresa Wirkkala, and Sally Cocovaunis for your friendship. The world would be a darker place without you.

Last but not least, thanks to my family: Mom, Dad, Deb and Dan Aldridge, Steve Graffius, and Jennifer and Jeff Cruzan for the right kind of love.

This book is about the power of forgiveness, love, courage, and dreams. Without these, our lives are nothing.

I hope you see yourself in these pages and dare to dream yourself into the future.

Here I go dreaming myself into the future and loving every minute of it...

Prologue 9
The Early Years 13
Blessings in a Storm 37
The Winds Bring Change 53
A Family Is Born 85
Winter's Thaw Rains Tears 97
The Awakening 117
New Beginnings 137
It Was Written in the Stars 163
One Moment in Time 175
The Next Generation 183
Epilogue 187

TABLE OF CONTENTS

PROLOGUE

The morning was dark as the storms rolled in and took back the start of the day. I sat by the window watching the trees whip back and forth from the strong winds. Thankfully, the house felt warm and safe, and I was glad to be inside on a day like today.

My own health had been slipping lately, and my body was tired. I took a good look at my reflection in the glass pane and wondered when all the aging snuck up on me and why I didn't take notice.

My hair was thin and gray, wrinkles lined my face, and my hands were worn from years of working outside.

I don't rightly know how old I am, not because I can't remember, but only because it never mattered. What was important was how I spent my days, not how many of them I had.

The rain started to come down hard now, and my reflection blurred as the raindrops pelted the glass.

"Tell us about growing up on the mountain," Jackson asked.

"What do you want to know?"

"Everything," he said excitedly, "but first, why don't folks call you by your real name?"

"Well, when I was a little girl, my mama always called me the Child. Maybe she always knew deep down in her heart that I was meant for someone else. Don't get me wrong. I always knew my given name, but it didn't seem to matter much. You see, I had no real life 'til I came to live on the mountain, and then I felt that I had been put on this earth to be everyone's child, Mattie's, Orange's, and Mama's."

Looking out the window, I watched the storm and figured today was a perfect day for remembering…

"Where do you want me to start?"

"At the beginning…"

"Well then, sit back and get comfortable. This could take a good while."

I turned my attention to my wood box and carefully unlatched the lid, opening up the world I remembered so well. My mind wandered back through the years 'til I came to the beginning. I unconsciously rubbed the green emerald and the memories came alive, like the stone did so many years ago ...

THE EARLY YEARS ...

Some folks say the day life begins is when you're in your mama's belly. Well, mine didn't. My life began the day I was dropped off at Mattie's house in the mountains of West Virginia. I was only a child, and it was the dead of night come one winter. There I stood, holding the few clothes I owned, freezing, and in my heart I knew my mama wasn't coming back this time. I knew this time was different.

Mattie said she found me on her front porch crying. She scooped me up in her arms like she had been waiting for me all her life and took me inside.

I felt a sense of relief, like I finally had come home, and I stopped crying.

I don't want to get ahead of myself, so let me start back to the days I remember living with my mama ...

I don't remember my mama much, just little things here and there that creep into my head sometimes. These memories I have are dusty and old, full of cobwebs reaching out to me as I try to take hold of them. Once in a while, I get hold of a thought that seems to run true, and I am grateful.

Like the time I remember sitting on my mama's bed as she was getting herself all dolled up. She was wearing a pretty dress with pink and white flowers on it, and she had on shoes that were shined up real bright and looked white as snow in the winter. Mama was smiling as she put on bright red lipstick, and she leaned over and kissed me on the forehead. I felt real special at that moment, like I was the center of her world. I like to think of that time, because most of the time I just felt lonely. I don't want you to think my mama didn't love me, because she did. I just think she didn't know how to care for me. I didn't fit into her world, and I'm not sure she fit into her world either. My mama's name was Viola, and it always reminded me of a flower. She seemed so delicate and fragile, maybe too much so, to be rearing a child of her own.

Anyhow, I remember driving around a lot in the automobile with Mama. Actually, I remember the feelings I had more than the actual drives, but I guess it's all the same anyway. Sometimes, when I hear old love songs, it pulls at my heart in ways I just don't understand. I figure it's a cobweb memory that always seems to vanish before I can get a firm grip on it.

My mama liked to drive, and as we bounced down the dusty mountain roads, I would get tired in the backseat and fall asleep to my mama's angelic voice singing one song after another. Truth be told, I remember waking up many times. It would be night-time, and I'd feel scared. Sometimes, I would stay bundled up in my blanket, not wanting to move, and I would play dead like some animals do to throw you off track. My mama would always come back for me though. Sometimes it would be the morning when the birds were chirping and the sun was out and ready to start the day. Other times it would still be dark, and I would wake up as car door squeaked open and my mama started the automobile. The engine always had a powerful sound when it came to life after sitting for a while.

You can see how, to this day, I get all kinds of feeling roaring up in my head when I drive in an automobile. It brings me back to the times before my life really began.

I guess you could say my memories are small, my feelings run deeper, and that's just how it is. Even though I didn't call Mattie my mama, she was the best thing that ever did happen to me. Mattie said my mama was a girl she knew growing up, and they were friends at school. She said my mama was real pretty with fair skin like a china doll, big brown eyes and long thick hair just like me. She lived with her family on a smaller piece of land closer to town. My mama talked a lot about leaving this town and never coming back. She told Mattie that her mama was beat down, and her daddy was good for nothing, who took advantage of her any time he could.

Well, I guess she meant what she said. She did run off one day and didn't come back for years. That is, 'til the day she came back home with me.

Mattie said she almost plum forgot about my mama until the day came when my mama dropped by out of the blue. My mama drove up the mountain one afternoon and talked about the old days like no time had passed between them. Mama spoke of the child she had and how she traveled far and wide looking for her own piece of heaven. I guess she never did find it, because there she was, back home again. She spoke of her folks and how old and feeble they had become. She said her brothers had moved on and had their own families now. Mattie said my mama seemed nervous and kept wringing her hands like she had some thoughts she wanted to share and just couldn't get the right words out.

Well, Mattie said she wasn't a bit surprised to find me two nights later on her porch crying. She said my mama was too restless to stay in this small town that held so many sad memories, and she must have headed out looking for some kind of peace. Mattie said she didn't question things she couldn't control and figured my mama would come back and get me when she was good and ready. Mattie said that when someone is trying to outrun their demons, it can take a good while. You see, Mattie was real smart about folks and said if it's God will, my mama would come back one of these days and claim me. I guess she wasn't good and ready. So I came to live with Mattie, and that's how my life really began.

I had my own room at the top of the house, and when it rained I could hear the noises right good, as the roof was metal. Mattie gave me my room way up top because the other room had Mammy and Pappy's old things in it. I liked my room, and sometimes I liked to dream I was sleeping in a bird's nest all the way on top of a tree. I didn't have the tree leaves or the stars overhead, but I liked to dream anyway. Being my room was up so high, I could see a long ways off, and sometimes at night, when the moon was showing off, I could see the pond shining real bright like a mirror.

Mattie always said, "It ain't right to be a show-off, as we are all just plain folk trying to get by," but I'm glad the moon shows off sometimes.

Mattie came from a family who used to work this very land. Her pappy was a drunk and sometimes did right by them and sometimes didn't. Her mammy was a God-fearing woman who took care of the children and prayed for better days. Mattie said she had a sister, but she was dead and buried a long time past.

For years she was real sick and her mammy couldn't make her any better. Mattie would call on her from time to time, as she had a cross with her name on it out in the clearing under a big 'ole oak tree. Right next to her sister was her mammy. Mattie says, "Life ain't fair, and the sooner you know it, the better off you'll be."

Thankfully, Mattie was the exact opposite of my mama and exactly what I needed. She was short, stout, and had brown hair that, most of the time, looked like a mess. Her large hands were rough and chapped from working the land, and her nails always had the mountain soil under them. Every day Mattie wore an old dress, the pattern faded from years of washings, and a flowered apron. The apron pockets always had a few shotgun shells and clothespins in them and were dirty from bending over in the garden day after day. Most mornings, she never even bothered to lace her boots, that way she could just step into them and start her day. You could tell by taking one look at her that she was a hard worker. Her face was weatherworn from working outside her entire life, and although she didn't have gentle features like my Mama, to me, she was beautiful.

Mattie went to school until fifth grade, but with her pappy gone a lot and her sister sick most of the time, Mattie had to help out her mammy working 'round the land. I didn't go to regular school, and in all the years I lived on the mountain, only one lady came a callin' about me. She was all dressed up fancy-like, driving an automobile, and looked kind of scared if you asked me.

Anyhow, Mattie said to mind myself and stay put, and that's what I did. Mattie just stood on the front porch, cradling her gun like a baby, and did not move one inch.

The school lady stayed by her automobile and said, "Will the child be attending school this year?"

"No, ma'am, this land is her school," said Mattie, a bit irritated.

"I have to disagree with you on that. She needs schooling so she'll grow up proper," said the woman.

Mattie said, "Ain't nobody telling me how to mind the child, and folks should mind their own business when it comes to rearing the little ones."

I didn't know if the lady agreed with Mattie or if the looks of Mattie with her trusty gun and dogs by her side changed her mind. Either way, we never did see that lady again, and Mattie continued schooling me the best way she saw fit.

*

Since Mattie grew up here, she knew most of the folks and knew what they said about her. Among other things, the town gossip was that she had her land booby trapped. That wasn't true, but that didn't matter much when it comes to folks talking. Mattie's pappy, at one time, did booby trap the property to keep away strangers from wandering on the property when he was on his travels. Mattie, on the other hand, although weary of strangers, didn't have the traps set out. Either way, Mattie had never been bothered by what the town folks had to say. She knew it was pure nonsense, and she always said, "I got better things to do with my time than waste it hanging out in the general store."

The local saloon was another place Mattie said men wasted their time, dulling their senses by drinking whiskey. "Just take a peek through the window sometime and see for yourself. Ain't no good ever come from drinking that firewater, and if you want to see what a wasted life looks like, that's the place."

Although I was afraid to see a wasted life, one day, my curiosity got the best of me and I walked to the edge of town to the saloon. I noticed some children sitting out front, and I asked them what they was doing.

"Waiting on our papa," they said.

"How come?" I asked.

"Mama makes us wait so we can help Papa get home."

"Don't your papa know where he lives?" I asked.

"Not after drinking whiskey all day he don't."

I figured the whiskey must be mighty powerful if grown men couldn't remember how to get home. Just then, a lady came out of the saloon pulling on her husband's shirt and cussing up a storm. "You is good for nothing, drinking whiskey when we is hungry!" she yelled as the baby cradled on her hip started to cry. It was a family like I had never seen before, and as they headed down the road, I heard that lady crying along with the little one.

I was shocked by the event, and as I looked to the kids lined up under the window, I took note that they didn't even blink an eye. I left that day not worrying about those men drinking their lives away, but instead, I was thinking about the little kids and how their papa was wasting their lives too. I never did walk down to the saloon again.

The town wasn't big, and you could walk from one end to the other in minutes. Most folks live tucked away in the mountains and have lived there for generations. We rarely got new blood moving in, and most folks just passed through on their way to somewhere more exciting. The police chief, Bobby Joe, kept a close eye on everyone moving through town and he seemed to know things before they even happened. The town jail had only two cells, and most of the time one was occupied by a local who had too much to drink. Bobby Joe would let him sleep it off and then send him home first thing in the morning, but not before Preacher Matthew had a chance to talk with him about his sinful ways. Bobby Joe used to give them scrambled eggs for breakfast, but when times got hard, all they got was burnt toast and a short sermon.

Bobby Joe did a fine job protecting our town, and he always found time to check in with the folks who lived farther out. Whenever he came a callin', he'd asked, "How y'all been? Need anything?" Mattie always said the same thing: "We don't need nothing from nobody." Mattie said charity is for the poor, and we ain't poor. I always thought Bobby Joe was sweet on Mattie, but she flatly denied that thinking. She said he's just lonely since his wife died a few years back. Seemed like everyone who was lonely always found a way to Mattie's just like I did. It made me wonder if she had a special sense for folks needing her or if it was the mountains that surrounded us and protected us like a mama bear protecting her young.

Although the town was a little tired looking, we had a mighty fine church. Even though the white paint was peeling off the boards, it still had a grand look about it. The steeple was tall, and at the very top was a large cross that you could see for miles in either direction. Windows on both sides of the church were opened up during service, and all through town you could hear the choir praising God through music as their songs filled the air with salvation. The church had wood floors that creaked as you walked over them, a testament to the years of worship among the town folk. Sometimes Mattie gave me a penny to put in the collection box so I could light a candle and pray for Mama.

Anyhow, Mattie and me worked real hard around the property, and never a day went by that we didn't have a ton of chores to do. Mattie tended to her garden like it was the babies she never did have. Every row was perfect, and we put out little signs that I got to color that showed what we were growing. Mattie had a special touch for tilling the soil, and everything we planted grew like it couldn't wait to peek out of the ground and meet us right away.

Mattie said our land was our own little haven from the outside world. We were well protected by a large wood gate that Mattie's pappy made back in the day when he traveled a good deal. Opening the gate was no easy task, especially in bad weather. It was heavy, and it usually took both of us to pull it across the road. Over the years, Mattie had wedged small tree limbs inside the wood frame for more privacy, and I added small rocks, tin scraps, and colored string to welcome anyone who came callin'. During the day the gate was kept open, but most nights we closed it for extra security.

Large trees lined the drive coming up the mountain, and as you came 'round the bend in the road, our house sat directly ahead, set back a bit against a lush forest. Our house was made of logs that Pappy downed his self, and we had a covered front porch that stretched from one end of the house to the other. The porch was set up on wood legs, and the dogs loved to sleep underneath when it was too hot outside. Three rocking chairs sat on the porch and were faded from years of use. Mattie always said ain't nothing can't be fixed if you just sit down for a spell and think on things. Anyway, we had an outhouse with a stone path, a small shed, barn, and a pond full of trout.

We were secluded, and you couldn't see our place from down the mountain; except for on the occasional day when the wind was blowing just right, you might have taken notice of the wisps of smoke coming up over the treetops from our chimney.

Our house wasn't fancy, but it was well built. Pappy added the upstairs loft bedroom for Mattie a few years after the house was finished. Being her sister was sick with God-knows-what kind of ailment, Mammy thought it was best if the girls didn't share a room. So they put a small iron bed upstairs with a wash stand for Mattie to keep her safe from the unknown germs her sister had. Mattie says she loved the room as much as I do.

Most everything we need we could get from the land, but sometimes Mattie traded what we had for something else we needed. That's when we traded with Orange. Orange was the traveling salesman, and he loved our peas and corn and took a bushel home every time he came a callin'. He said they were the sweetest thing he ever did taste, and that always seemed to make Mattie beam with pride. I never did know anyone before with a name like Orange. It's a funny name by itself, but when I met Orange for the first time, it suited him just fine.

In fact, about the only person Mattie didn't try to scare away with her gun was Orange. Mind you, Mattie still kept her gun ready, swung up over her shoulder, but she always left the front porch and made her way to his automobile all polite-like. Mattie said that mountain folk need to be ready for all kinds of trouble. Every now and then it's the weather, animals, or even other mountain folk, but either way, you can't let your guard down, 'cause that's when trouble comes a callin'.

Anyhow, this one day I will never forget. It was a day that trouble did come a callin', and it was a good thing Mattie was ready.

Orange came calling one morning, and things just seemed wrong from the get-go. I don't know if it was the clouds swirling in the sky or the way the wind was creeping through the trees real sneaky-like. Maybe it was the nervous twitches Orange was having, but I tell you what, Mattie always says to trust your own senses, and my senses was telling me something was wrong. I think Mattie was listening to her senses too, because she told me to keep close and moved real careful-like, making her way closer to Orange.

First off, Mattie asked Orange how the day was panning out, and he said that he had some trouble down at the Parsons' land. I have to tell you at this point in the story that the Parsons is one mean bunch and all they are is trouble. If they ain't in trouble, they are making the trouble—the oldest one in particular. He looked like he'd never taken a bath or washed his clothes. Long, greasy hair stuck to the sides his pale face, and he always had dark circles under his eyes from drinking. Although he was a scrawny one, he was the one to watch out for. The police chief him-self will say that family is as wild as the blackberries growing in the mountains, and he can't tame them any better than he can stop the berries from taking over whatever lies in their path.

So, as soon as Mattie asked what happened, I had the feeling the first piece of the puzzle for the day had been laid in place and there was no going back now. Orange told Mattie how, when he went calling on the Parsons, the boys was acting like a stirred-up hornets' nest right from the get-go.

He said he wished he'd never have stopped, but it was too late, as he was already there and out of the automobile. Come to find out, they had been up the better part of the night drinking whiskey, and they was still drunk and all riled up when Orange came callin'. The older boy, the pack leader, so to speak, accused Orange of cheating them on their last deal.

"The way I see's it, you got to make things right by me," the Parson boy said, slurring his words as the younger boys looked on and snickered.

"I ain't done no wrong by you, not then or not ever," Orange said calmly.

"That's not the way I see things … I see you trying to steal from me and now you got's to take what's comin' to you—."

Orange said he slowly started inching his way backward, hoping the good-for-nothing drunks would pay no mind. Well, they did pay mind and whipped themselves into a fury like the clouds overhead, and before he knew it, he said they came at him like a pack of wild dogs.

"The younger boys grabbed me from behind while the older boy landed a punch square on my jaw, and that's when I started fearing for my life," said Orange.

"Oh, Lord have mercy … You know them boys is rotten to the core, Orange," said Mattie, matter-of-factly. "You're lucky they didn't beat you silly!"

"I know Miss Mattie, but a man's got to make a living, and I was always real careful dealing with them. This time was different though. This time I knew I was in trouble the minute I got there."

Anyhow, he went on to say that, thankfully, they was weak from whiskey, riled up, but weak, and after a small scuffle, he made it to his automobile and lit outta that place.

Mattie and me then looked at Orange and noticed how dirty his clothes were and how he had blood on his cheek and hands.

No sooner than he got done telling his story, we heard ruckus from down the road, and I knew right then and there the second piece of the puzzle was laid in place. Mattie took one look at me and said to run to the house and grab Pappy's shotgun off the wall. "Hurry, Child," she said as she fingered how many shells she had in the pocket of her flowered apron. Orange got a worried look on his face and ran to the trunk where he normally kept his treasures for sale, except this time, he dug down deep and come up with his own shotgun. Nobody was talking, but we all knew that the Parsons weren't allowed on this land since way back when Mattie's folks had a run-in with the Parson folks.

I had a lot of thoughts running in my head as I ran to the house, but I felt like things was moving real slow, like a dream or something. I pulled the chair over to the wall and stood on it to get Pappy's shotgun. It was real heavy and felt cold and smooth in my hands, like it had been mine all along. As I jumped down, I saw out the corner of my eye Mattie and Orange armed and ready for whatever was coming our way. I had a quick flutter in the pit of my stomach, and I said a silent prayer for all of us. Mattie always says that God knows the good ones from the bad ones, and I was hoping God was paying attention right here, right now. I walked quick, but careful, back down the porch and to Mattie when I saw the first boy round the bend. Mattie looked at me as she tossed me two more shells and told me real serious-like to put those in my pocket. The older Parson boy walked like he had a purpose, with his gun slung over his shoulder while the other three just followed like the obedient dogs they were.

Before they could figure out what kind of trouble they wanted to stir up, Mattie called out to them … , "Get off my property—you ain't welcome here and never have been!"

That stopped the older one in his tracks as the nips to the bottle had slowed his thinking down a bit, and they was never a bright bunch to begin with.

Mattie took this silence as a show of weakness and told them, "Whatever beef you got with Orange ain't got nothin' to do with me. So if you're look-ing for trouble today, you found it trespassing on my land!"

The older one now held his shotgun with a firm grip and said, "Why are you protecting a negro? That's just like you. Always thinking you know bet-ter than the rest of the town folk. But you ain't better. You couldn't even have your own baby, so you had to keep someone else's bastard child."

Mattie's jaw clenched as she said, "Ain't nothing 'bout the way I live my life is your concern, and I think you best head back home, boy."

I figure the fight they was looking for now wasn't about Orange no more, but about Mattie and me. It was at that same moment that I felt the earth shift and the third piece of the puzzle fell into place. The younger Parson boy toting a shotgun and shaking like a leaf on a tree fired off his gun and hit Mattie in the arm, dropping her to her knees in one split second.

I screamed as loud as I could, and even though I was scared to death, I had my wits about me and fired Pappy's shotgun true as could be. Mattie always told me when we was hunting to take care of the big-gest and most dangerous animal first …

So that's what I did.

I took out the older boy, who was the pack leader, and shot him clean through the chest. The look in his eyes was fixed as he fell to the ground. The other boys were confused, and it was like someone had glued their boots to the ground. I saw Orange out the corner of my eye, and he still had not said a word and never flinched neither. He turned his gun and aimed it at the boy who had fired the shot, ready to fire if the boy so much as moved.

Mattie was bleeding from her wound as she told me in a thick voice to run down the mountain and fetch the chief.

"I can't leave you, Mattie—"

"You got to. Hurry along, Child."

I looked to Orange, who gave me a nod, and so I ran through the woods, taking the worn paths I knew by heart. I wasn't thinking straight and I wasn't confused either. It's like this day was doomed from the get-go, and now all the pieces of the puzzle had come together.

I fetched the police chief like Mattie said and I told him my story. He said "Them Parson boys went ahead and did it this time" and took me back home. He put me in the back seat and wrapped me in a blanket. Even though I felt like I was burning up, I couldn't stop my body from shaking. As we drove up the mountain in the police cruiser, I listened to the songs I knew too well playing in my head, and this time I thought about Mattie. She told me once that there is a time in everyone's life when you have to play the cards you are dealt, even though you don't want to. She said life sometimes makes a grand entrance to show you who is boss...I figured this was my time.

As you can well might imagine, Mattie refused to see the town doc, but Bobby Joe wouldn't take no for an answer. Mattie, being weak from her injury, gave in and let him send for Doc Austin. We was all thanking the good Lord as the buckshot only hit her upper arm and it could have been a lot worse. I watched Mattie's face as the doc picked one pellet after another out of her arm, and although she looked pale and shaken, she never shed so much as one tear.

Sadly, the older Parson boy died right there on our land, but there would be no cross laid for him under the 'ole oak tree. Strangely, to this day, I never did know his first name, and I never want to neither. I killed a young man, and for this I knew I would be judged, but I also knew I would do the same thing again to protect Mattie.

Bobby Joe said the boys were trespassing and no trouble would come our way. Orange said he was forever indebted to me and Miss Mattie for showing such bravery, and he has been our good friend ever since. He said hard times can bring people together in ways that real kin never can. Mattie healed right good, but I can't say the same for the Parson clan. Their pack leader was gone, and the younger boys, not used to having their own thoughts, were lost without him.

Thankfully, a short time later, they were all gone from the mountain. Come to find out, the bank took back their house and Bobby Joe said they packed up in the middle of the night and headed out west. Other than the occasional squatters, the house stood empty and dark as a reminder of lives wasted.

I had bad dreams for a while after life made its grand entrance. Dreams that left me scared as the day the Parson boys came on our land.

One dream had me running down the mountain from a pack of wild wolves. *They were right on my heels, and I felt their hot, short breaths against my legs. Steam rose from their nostrils as they chomped down, biting only the cool air between us. The fear of being pulled to the ground by their powerful jaws kept me one step ahead of them, and as I glanced back, I saw angry eyes that pierced the darkness like a knife.*

Every time I had this dream, I woke with a fright, drenched in sweat, and I could still smell the fear in my room.

I now know what Mattie meant when she said life's not always fair. Sometimes, when the wind is lazy or the clouds are dancing in the sky, I remember the feeling in the air like it was yesterday, and I just close my eyes and pray for lighter thoughts.

It took some time for things to get back to normal on the mountain. Mattie had her arm in a sling for a good while, so I had to help her with tending to the garden and feeding the animals. I didn't mind, as I felt safe by Mattie's side, and I needed that feeling now more than ever. One night as we sat by the fire, I said to Mattie, "I was scared you was going to die and I'd be left all alone on the mountain."

"Child, it would take a lot more than some silly 'ole buckshot to take me away from you!"

I believed her. From the bottom of my heart, I knew she was telling me the truth.

It was a while before we made our way back into town after the Parson trouble. We had supplies to buy and some to trade. Mattie didn't much like driving the old truck, and when we started it up that morning, it sounded cold and tired. It shook and sputtered for a few minutes before the engine finally sounded steady. Mattie put the shotgun on the back rack and we loaded the truck bed with bushels of corn, peas, eggs, and apple pies. Everything was tied down for a secure ride down the bumpy road to town.

Once in town, we made our way to the local merchant who traded our goods for things like sugar, flour, kerosene, and coffee. Mattie's pies were always a hit, and some of the local town folk who would hang out in the store for the better part of the day always enjoyed a slice. The general store had a couple of tables set back in the corner where the old men smoked and played checkers for hours on end. Seems to me they just hung out to hear all the "goings on" with the town folk. They were worse than the women when it come to town gossip. Sometimes, I would hear them talk about my mama, and they thought just because I was a child, my ears didn't hear.

Today, I heard whispers about our troubles with the Parson boys. Mind you, nobody liked them boys, but that didn't matter. They watched us like we was some kind of carnival freaks rolling through town for the first time.

Mattie noticed the attention we was attracting and pulled me aside. "Pay them no mind, Child. Folks that spend that much time talking about others don't have enough love or work in their own lives."

So, it was from that day on that I looked upon them with pity instead of having thoughts of shaking some sense into them.

Mattie hauled a big bag of flour and some sugar to the truck while I read the town postings tacked up by the front door. Most of the postings were messages for loved ones, and sometimes, as folks passed through town, they would leave a message for other kin to let them know which direction they were headed. Some folks were stranded and needed help with food or gasoline to keep moving. It was all a reminder to me that times were hard and I was blessed to have the life I had.

Mattie and me worked our way through town taking care of our business. Mattie was never one to be idle, and she approached her town outings just as she did all her other chores, with efficiency and ease. We stopped by the post office to see if we had any mail. We never had any, and we didn't that day either. I always wondered if one day my mama might send me a postcard from her travels. She never has, and sadly, I don't hold my breath about it either.

Mattie and I headed back home through the winding roads up the mountain. As we drove, I wondered why so many folks seemed lost in a town where they grew up.

I asked Mattie about this and she said some folks just don't have the thoughts to carry them into the coming years. She said folks can lose themselves if they quit dreaming. Mattie said her pappy was a dreamer when he didn't let the bottle take over his thoughts. He would travel around the mountain range, sometimes working, but mostly trading. Sometimes he would be gone for quite a spell and her mammy would have to tend to the girls and the land all by herself. He would come home with wild stories about mining for gold. Mattie said her mammy told her not to believe such tales, as it was the whiskey talking. One thing for sure, he was a "saver" like Mattie, and she said it was the one thing they had in common.

Mattie said one day, her pappy never did come home. He left in late summer one year and would usually come home at the first sign of winter. That year he didn't. Mattie said she prayed real hard for his return, and when he still had not come home by springtime, she knew something bad must have happened.

"Was you scared, Mattie, when your Pappy didn't come home?" I asked.

"I was scared, but I had to be brave for Mammy. I told her we would be fine, but after that, she never was the same again. Some of the town folk talked about how he'd run off was all, but as much as Pappy liked his adventures, we knew it wasn't true. Pappy would never leave us, that I was sure. Times got even harder for us after that. Mammy took care of the house and my sister while I worked the land all by myself. Not long after Pappy went missing, my sister took a turn for the worse, and months later she passed. Mammy was crushed, and many days she never even got out of bed. It was heartbreaking to watch, and I felt all alone. One evening, I heard Mammy saying her nightly prayers and she asked to be reunited with Pappy and my sister. She cried as she said I could take care of myself, but my sister was weak with illness and needed her Mama. Mind you, I wasn't upset from knowing this … she was a good mama and her loyalty stood with the one who needed her most. That had never been me, even after my sister died. Though she eventually got back to working alongside me on the land, she always had a faraway look in her eye … "

"Then one day, while she was hanging out the wash, she fell to the ground never to wake again. I think her heart finally gave out from all the grief she had suffered. She was ready … had been ready for years I reckon, and I could swear she had a smile on her face as I cradled her in my arms for the last time."

"Oh, Mattie, I am so sorry," I said.

"Me too, Child."

We drove up the mountain in silence, as there was nothing more to say and we both knew it. Those days were gone, and there was not a thing either one of us could do to change it.

BLESSINGS IN
THE STORM

Seemed like it was no time at all before fall was setting in and it was time for Mattie and me to prepare for the long winter months ahead. Our days were busy storing food, chopping wood, curing meat, and canning. Orange called on us and was always willing to lend a hand in trade for a nice hot meal. He would stay for hours, helping us haul wood to the back porch or bringing in water from the well. I never saw him wear nothing but overalls, a white shirt, and a black jacket. His hat was black and broke in from years of wear and his shoes looked like they had been repaired many times like mine. His overalls were frayed at the bottom and although his jacket had seen better days, he would take off the coat real careful-like and fold it over the rocker on the front porch. He'd then roll up the sleeves of his shirt and get to work with the same attention Mattie gave to her chores.

I never did know if he had a family waiting for him somewhere or if he was a dreamer like Mattie's pappy and just kept on the move. Either way, we liked him a lot. He seemed to drop by more often, and Mattie always found work for him. It happened to be that one day he came by, a storm was brewing. It looked like it was going to be a fierce one, and the sky was darkening as we finished hauling wood to the back porch. Mattie said that Orange better get going, as it would be hard driving down the mountain. Quickly, she packed him a small supper to take with him as Orange put on his suit coat and readied his automobile.

Within the hour, the wind picked up and the storm showed its true strength as the skies opened up and roared like a great beast. Mattie and me just finished closing the shutters on the windows and getting all the animals safe for the night when the rain started strong and steady. Mattie says life has its own rhythm, and this storm was no different. It sounded like a great ballad with the steady beat of the thunder rolling through the open sky, and the backdrop of lightning flashes illuminated the valley below.

Mattie and me settled in for the night and ate supper in front of a roaring fire to keep us warm. The fireplace was impressive, made of river rock, and had been built by Mattie's pappy. He added a large mantel made from a large downed oak tree and sanded the edges until they were smooth. Every year, we hung our Christmas stockings from nails that had been long ago pounded into the wood. I felt warm and full inside as I curled up with a book. Mattie settled in and got to knitting a blanket that she was nearing done. Before I knew it, my eyes got heavy, and I was lulled to sleep by the steady click of her knitting needles.

We woke the next morning to a beautiful sunrise and a crisp, fresh scent in the air. I set about collecting the morning eggs and feeding the animals as Mattie started breakfast. The very thought of bacon frying in the skillet made me work faster as my stomach ached for my favorite meal.

The hours passed and soon after lunch we heard Orange's automobile coming round the bend. Being he was just here yesterday, we were a bit surprised to see him again. Come to find out Orange's house was hit by lightning in last night's storm and he had no place to go. The house was in ruins, and Orange had saved what he could and hauled it in his automobile. He said most of his worldly possessions had either been burnt or soaked from the heavy rains.

"You're welcome to stay in our old shed for a spell," Mattie offered.

"Oh, I sure don't want to impose, Miss Mattie," Orange replied.

"That's pure nonsense, Orange!" she said as she set about unloading his things before he could put up a fuss. "We can always use another set of hands 'round here to help out. Besides, this ain't charity by any means."

This seemed to put his mind at ease. "I'm sure grateful for your hospitality, Miss Mattie."

We worked the rest of the day cleaning out the shed and moving pappy's old things to the house. Back in the day, Mattie said her pappy would spend hours out there tinkering with one thing or another. This had been his private place where he dreamed big dreams and nipped on the bottle, hidden away from Mammy's scornful eyes. The shed, so long neglected, had a musty and dank smell. The dirt floor was uneven but smooth, and I swept it just like I was sweeping the wood floors in the main house. There was an old wood stove to keep Pappy warm on the cold winter eves, but it now had cobwebs that reached out to the wood beams above. On the work bench, there was an assortment of tools and whiskey crates filled with pappy's findings from all his travels. Rummaging through the odds and ends, I found some old burlap sacks that I could stuff with hay and make a fresh bed for Orange. The shack had one window, and straight across on the other wall, a fern had taken root and was growing up out of the ground. I figured if something could live under these conditions, I had no right to disturb it.

Orange moved in the few belongings he had saved, and by the end of the day, the shed had the look of a home. We started a fire, filled the kerosene lanterns hanging from the ceiling, and Orange laid down a rug from his old kitchen. I must say, the 'ole shed had taken on a new life, and Orange seemed content with his new surroundings.

The following morning Orange got up early in the morning to help me with chores before he set out peddling his wares. He had to go over on the other side of the mountain and would be back by supper. As the sun was rising over the mountaintop, Orange was already heading down the mountain.

Mattie and me worked all morning washing clothes and tending to the animals and our garden. By noon, we sat for a spell on the front porch, and within minutes we heard the sound of a car headed up the mountain. Mattie reached over for her shotgun that was leaning against the house and sat it across her lap, all the while rocking in her chair. Bobby Joe rounded the bend in his police car and we were able to relax. He parked his car, tipped his hat, and said good afternoon. Mattie offered him some hot tea and he seemed pleased for the invite, as we all headed inside for warmth. Mattie heated the water and we all sat down at the kitchen table. Bobby Joe said he heard that Orange's house had been hit by lightning and was in ruins. "That's right," said Mattie.

"Do you happen to know where's he staying?"

"Sure do," said Mattie. "Right here, if you must know."

Bobby Joe looked worried about these facts and rubbed his forehead as he gave this some thought. "I don't know if that's such a good idea, Mattie," he said.

Nothing gets Mattie fired up more than folks minding other people's business.

She poured the tea as she said, "Bobby Joe, what I do with my life ain't nobody's concern. I can hire who I like when I like. I like Orange and always have. He will be bunking in Pappy's old shed while he is here. For God's sake, the man lost his home and all his belongings … what would you expect me to do?"

Bobby Joe said he understood, but he was worried. Mattie dismissed his worries with a flick of her hand, and that was that. Bobby Joe headed out that afternoon, knowing Mattie could fend for herself, and he couldn't do a thing to change her mind once she decided on something.

That evening, Orange came home by suppertime, and I took a hot meal to the shed for him. He seemed pleased and thanked me for my kindness. He said we was good folks and he felt blessed by knowing us. I didn't know a whole lot about Orange, and he didn't talk a lot, but I knew I liked him.

Morning after morning, Orange would wake before sunrise and help me with chores. We got into a routine, and little by little, Orange talked and we learned more about each other. I found out he had no family on the mountain, and his parents were long dead. He did have three older brothers, but he had no idea where they were or if they was still living. Times were really hard and folks did what they needed to do, to make ends meet, and for a lot of folks, that meant looking elsewhere for work.

Anyhow, his house that got struck by lightning was small and run down, and he had lived there for years. It had been abandoned years before, and it only had one bedroom, a small kitchen, and a front room. He said the roof leaked and the cold air would sneak in between the boards, leaving him cold all winter long. Orange tried his best to keep the cold away by stuffing rags and newspaper into the cracks between the boards, but it only helped a little. I was glad to hear how much he liked the shed, and he said he was more comfortable there, as it kept him cozy warm. He said his bones ached sometimes from the harsh winters, and his bad leg felt better today than it had in years.

*

Sometimes folks who passed through the area would try to squat on the lower part of our property along the mountains. They would build small shelters up against the rock ridge to keep them out of the wind and the dust. Although Mattie was sympathetic, we worried about the possible problems that came along with their troubles. There was a good many folks still trying to live day by day. We shared what we could from our garden, but Mattie always made it clear that was all we had. She did not want folks coming up the mountain or staying longer, knowing we had food.

So that's why most evenings, Orange would help me pull the gate closed to discourage folks from coming up the mountain. We felt truly blessed to have our few acres to protect us and provide us with enough food to live off the land. We never got used to seeing children with no shoes, hungry and filthy, following behind their parents with a blank look in their eyes.

Orange said we had to be careful, and we tried to stay on the mountain and only go into town when absolutely necessary. We always kept a loaded shotgun with us, and Mattie told me never to wander around the mountain by myself.

As times continued to be tough for most folks, Orange worked a little more around our place instead of being gone all day. When we had extra eggs or vegetables from our garden, me and Orange would sell them at the bottom of the road. Although we had enough food to feed us and wood to keep us warm, we always were in need of money for things like kerosene or gasoline. Butter, sugar, salt, and flour were also a must, and a cup of coffee was the thing that got Mattie going in the morning.

We never made much money, but every little bit helped. Mattie did not believe in banks, and when a lot of folks lost their savings, Mattie did not. Although she never had a lot of money, she was lucky to at least still have her money, and it was hid right there on our property. I never knew exactly where it was hid and I never asked.

Thankfully, we came to find out that Orange was real good at repairing things. He was able to fix things around the barn that had been in disrepair for years. Everything was re-used and nothing was ever thrown away. One day, Orange noticed our shoes were in bad shape and offered to help fix them too. Mattie's shoes were split all the way down the sides and held together with string. Orange cut the string off, and with some leather laces he found in his supplies, he sewed the bottom of the sole to the top. He then put a new piece of leather inside the boots and even shined them up real nice-like. They didn't look new by any means, but they felt new. Mattie was so pleased not to be digging small rocks out of her shoes all day.

Mine, on the other hand, were worn out right through the sole of the boot. I had holes under each foot on each shoe. Orange put leather in mine too, but it was a little thicker. My foot didn't fit as well in the shoe, but Orange said to give it some time and it would be fine. At least my feet were dry, and that was something.

As the snow began to thaw and the days became warmer, we worked outside more and more. Every year, our garden yielded more and more food, and that was a good thing, because we had one more mouth to feed with Orange living here. I hoped Orange would not want to move on when the weather improved. Thankfully, he never mentioned it, and neither did we.

Mattie and me loved having him around. He said he loved Miss Mattie's cooking and was gonna get fat from all her good cooking and baking. Actually, we all looked like we could gain some weight, but especially Orange. He was so tall and skinny and still walked with a slight limp. I didn't know how tall he was, but he was at least six feet tall. His overalls hung on his body like he hadn't eaten in ages. Funny thing though, he was real strong and was a great help to Mattie and me.

And so after the first year of living together, we all fell into a routine and worked hard to provide for each other. Orange was very protective of us, and we felt the same toward him. We spent many an afternoon reading on the front porch, and it was on one of those days we had an unexpected visitor. We saw her before we heard anything, as she was on foot. Orange turned to me and said, "Child, looks like we have company coming our way." He gestured toward the road.

I squinted to get a better look, as I had no idea who this person was. Orange called out to Mattie and said, "Miss Mattie, we got us some company." Mattie reached for her gun and walked out the front porch screen, already looking down the road. Orange kept rocking in the chair, curious about who would come calling on foot.

The woman was tired and walked up the road with a deep weariness in each step she took. She wore a tattered dress, worn-out shoes, and had dark, tanned skin that looked like leather from the sun. She stopped before reaching the porch and that's when Mattie asked, "What is it you need today?"

It's then that the woman pointed toward Orange and said, "Ma'am, I come to see him."

Well, as you can imagine, Orange wasn't expecting that, and as he stood, he said, "Well, come up out of the sun then and sit for a spell." Orange gestured toward the other rocking chair, and the woman hesitated, looking at Mattie, unsure what to do. Mattie nodded her head and turned to go back inside. I got up off the steps and joined Mattie inside the house. Too curious to stop myself, I peeked out the porch screen door as the woman sat down, and I wondered who she was and why she was calling on Orange.

Mattie said we should get some tea for the woman, as she looked mighty parched. I quickly helped Mattie with the drinks and hurried back out on the porch to see what I was missing. As I neared the woman with the tea, she looked so shocked. I figured she really was parched and maybe even a little delirious. I handed her the cup and she just stared at it like she didn't know what it was.

Orange watched the exchange between me and the woman with a funny smirk on his face before he said, "Thank Miss Mattie for the tea, Child. It sure do look refreshing ... "

"Yes sir-ee," he said. "Mighty refreshing."

Reluctantly I went back inside and sat down by the screen door. Mattie said, "Child, ain't none of that your business." I agreed with Mattie on that, yet I couldn't move from my spot as I waited for the woman to speak.

Orange just sat in that rocker and drank his tea, rocking back and forth, not saying a word and waiting for the woman to say her piece. After she seemed to catch her breath, the woman said her name was Tess, and she came to deliver some sober news. She went on to say she was here on behalf of her sister, who married Orange's brother. She said, "Orange, your big brother Bo died a while back out west. He left behind a wife and four little ones. My sister sent me word and said to find you and tells you. So, here I am."

The air seemed to get heavy around us as Orange put his face in his hands and said, "Lord have mercy ... "

I watched as Orange sat silently with his thoughts, and I could tell he was struggling with his memories.

Minutes passed before Orange finally said, "Tess, I thank you kindly for going out of your way to deliver such news. I am saddened to hear this. Yes, ma'am, saddened indeed."

Orange always had a quiet way about him, and although he wasn't a big talker, he had many a thoughts that he just kept to himself. I could tell his heart was sad just by looking into his eyes. He called out to me, knowing I must be right close, and said, "Child, I gots to drive Tess back home. Let Miss Mattie know I'll be back before nightfall."

It was then as he got up out of the rocking chair that I noticed his leg quivering a bit more than usual. Orange looked kind of shaky and frailer than he had before the lady came a callin'. Tess thanked me kindly for the tea and followed Orange down the steps.

I didn't know what it felt like to have someone you love die, but I did know the feeling of having a loved one gone, and it didn't feel so good. Orange came back that night by suppertime and I took him his food to the shed. He seemed tired as he told me the woman was headed out west to join her sister. I had some mixed feelings about the passing of his brother, because I worried if that meant he was going to leave us.

With my head drooped and wringing my hands, I spoke just above a whisper and said, "Orange, does you feel the need to go out west too?"

"Child, West Virginia is all I know … my life is here in these mountains. I don't know nothing different. Anyhow, I can't leave you and Miss Mattie with so much work needing to be done 'round this place." He winked at me and smiled, and then said, "No, Child, too much work to be done, that's for sure."

I let out a sigh of relief before I said, "How long has it been since you seen your brother?"

"It's been a good while … years I reckon. When I was a young'n, he would watch over me when my Mama washed clothes for the white folks. Bo was only a year older than me, and folks always thought we was twins, until I hurt my leg. Then they didn't think that no more … "

"How did you hurt your leg, Orange?"

"I hurt it one day working in the fields. Bo always blamed himself being he was right there, but sometimes it ain't no one's fault. Things just happen … "

Orange's voice trailed off, and I could tell how sad he was remembering the old days. Slowly, I got up and said goodnight. I could tell Orange needed to be alone with his thoughts.

That evening, I sat with Mattie and told her I had been nervous Orange would leave us for his brother's family. Mattie said she understood my worries, having the same fear herself. "We are like a family. If Orange left, I would be very sad indeed," said Mattie.

Curling up to Mattie, I couldn't help but think how none of us was blood kin, yet our bonds grew tighter every passing day we spent together.

That night, I dreamed of a lone wolf standing on the crest behind our house. *The long, deep howls woke me and I crept quietly to my window. I pulled open the curtains and felt the breeze upon my face, and as I looked out into the night, I saw a full moon awash in a deep orange color. The darkness of the night and the light com-*

ing off the moon were in perfect harmony. For whatever reason, I thought the wolf was there just for me, as well as the moon. It was a beautiful evening, and I stood at the window for a good while, taking it all in.

The next morning I smiled as I rose from bed, remembering my dream, knowing it was special. I did not tell Mattie or Orange about my dream. I figured some things weren't meant to be shared.

Orange worked alongside us most of that summer and started to spend less and less time traveling. At first he would come home earlier than usual, but after a while, he started staying home most of the day. As the seasons passed, we clung to each other as the only family we ever knew. We were content and happy and looked upon each day as a gift and not something to be wasted. Orange always had good ideas about things we could do to make a few cents, and this helped out quite a bit when it come to affording supplies like sugar, salt, and such. With Orange helping out more around the place, Mattie even found time to go fishing with me every so often, which I loved.

Funny how time goes by so quickly, and before you know it, years passed. Well, that's how it was.

Mattie once told me time treats everybody the same. It's yours to waste or do something good with. I felt that we had spent ours wisely. We shared with others when possible and worked hard to keep a roof over our heads.

THE WINDS BRING CHANGE

One morning when the air was cool and a slight breeze carried the clouds quickly overhead, I should have read the skies and known today was going to be something different; something different than all the other days since my life began.

I started with my morning chores as usual, with Orange by my side helping. We fed the chickens, and as we brought up wood to the back porch, Mattie was hanging out the morning laundry on the clothesline. The shirts were flapping gently in the wind like they had something to say. I should have listened. As it was, the first thing I heard was an automobile coming up the road. Mattie, never far from her shotgun, picked it up where it lay by the clean wash, and walked out to the front of the house to see who was headed our way. The car that rounded the bend was not one we had seen before. Mattie's voice, carried by the breeze, called out and said, "Orange, you keep the child close to you, ya hear?"

Orange said, "Yes, Miss Mattie, don't you worry 'bout a thing."

The automobile parked and shook violently as the engine shut off. Mattie stood cradling her gun as she watched the car door open, and when the dust settled she found herself face to face with an old friend. Now, I did not know who this woman was, but Orange sensed something and put his arm over my shoulder, pulling me closer.

The woman looked in my direction and seemed to melt a little at the mere sight of me.

Mattie then said, "It's been a while, hasn't it, Viola?"

"Yes, Mattie, it has."

"Well then, you might as well come and sit for a spell," she said as she motioned to the front porch.

Mattie sat in one rocker and the woman sat in the other. Orange and I walked over and stood at the steps, not sure what was going on.

Mattie then said, "Child, I don't reckon I know how to say this, so I will just come out and say it. This here is, your mama."

Well, I must say, my legs buckled and Orange, sensing my weakness, held me just a bit firmer to keep me from falling down the steps. Mattie got up and took my arm, guiding me to the rocker she had been sitting in. My head felt confused while my heart was racing a mile a minute.

I looked to the woman, hoping it would stir up in me some distant memories, but to tell you the truth, I wouldn't have known that she was my mama if I passed her in town. She was wearing a flowered dress with large brown buttons running up the front. Her hat was brown, and her hair was pinned back behind it. Her shoes were white and dirty like they had traveled a long ways to get here. She had two bruises on her leg that were turning yellow, and a fresher one on her arm that still showed off its bright purple coloring. Finally, I looked into her eyes as she fidgeted, watching me watch her. I took a big, dry gulp and said, "Pleased to meet you."

She said, "Child, I missed you. Come give your mama a big hug."

Reluctantly, I gave her a hug, and as she held me close, my mind was miles away.

She pulled me back and took a long look at me and said, "You look just like me when I was your age," while tears ran down her cheeks.

I heard her talking about how much I had grown and something about the years just slipping by, but

I was only half listening. I was still trying to under-stand how minutes before, my life was safe and nor-mal, and now I was sitting on the porch with the woman I thought about for so many years. So many nights, I would lie awake and wonder if she found her place in the world. Now she was right next to me and I didn't know what to do or say.

Orange then excused himself, saying something about how he had work to finish up in the barn. I watched him walk away and I had the strong urge to follow him. With every step he took my heart sank, and I felt more alone than I had ever felt in my life.

I looked at Mattie, who sensed my sadness, and she said, "How about we get some tea for your mama?" We left Mama on the porch alone, and I sheepishly fell in line behind Mattie. Once inside, I told Mattie I was scared 'bout my mama being here, and I didn't know how to act or what to do.

Mattie said, "Child, she come to see you and we got to welcome her, as it must have been hard for her after all these years."

"What if she is here to claim me and take me away from you and Orange?"

"Let's not dream up any worries right now. One thing at a time, Child … one thing at a time."

As I numbly helped Mattie with the tea, I tried to hide my trembling hands and worried thoughts. As we walked back to the porch, I saw my mama wiping her dirty shoes with a white handkerchief, which she shyly tucked back in her dress. My memo-ries of her primping for nights in town came flooding back to me, and I felt small again—too small to be dealing with such a big day in my life.

Mattie pulled over the other rocker and we all sat down to talk.

My mama spoke first, saying, "Child, I missed you terribly and have thought of you every day since I been gone. I know I haven't done right by you. I just didn't know how to care for you. You see, Child, this town wasn't the best place for me to be living, but I knew it would be good for you. I knew Mattie would care for you in ways I just couldn't."

Mama then pulled out the same handkerchief that she wiped her shoes with and now dabbed at her eyes. She was wringing her hands, and as she tried to form her next thoughts, I looked out toward the barn and saw Orange glancing our way while tinkering with something. We locked eyes and there was no need for words. I knew he was with me and it calmed my heart down a beat or two, which I sorely needed. I then looked at the two women sitting to my right. One gave me birth and the other was the only mama I had ever really known. I never thought I would see this day, and because of that, I was having a real hard time trying to figure out what to say. I knew how much I loved Mattie, but when I looked at my mama, I could tell how difficult this was for her too. My loyalties were being tested already, and although I wondered all these years about my mama, a part of me now wished this day had never come. I looked to Mattie and saw in her eyes true sympathy for my mama.

With a new sense of myself, I looked at the woman who gave me birth and felt compassion. She did not know the kind of peace in her heart that I did. Yet, she gave me the greatest gift any one person could give another; she gave me a family. Her tears now made me thankful because her sacrifices gave me a new life. My heart ached for her for the first time, and I prayed silently for God to take her hand and give her what she longed for.

It was at that same instant she reached for my hand and held it tight.

The air seemed to sizzle around us and I understood everything at that moment. It's like the time I saw a preacher man put his hand on the forehead of sinners and those wracked with pain to free them of their burdens. God was using that preacher man to help heal folks, and I figured God was working through me and needed me to help heal my mama's heart. My mama needed me to comfort her. Funny how a child must do the consoling, but I had something in my heart that she never did have. My inner self was stronger than hers, as I had the love of a family. I looked her deeply in the eyes and thanked her from the bottom of my heart for bringing me to Mattie's. She cried and cried, and I knew I had said the thing she needed most to hear.

Mattie sat there watching us as if she was in some kind of trance. She, too, dabbed at her eyes with her apron and thanked the Lord above for the peaceful look that come over my mama's face. It was as if a heavy burden had been lifted and tossed aside.

My mama said, "Child, I never forgave myself for leaving you, even though I knew it was best."

"No need to forgive yourself, Mama," I said. "I never had bad feelings toward you. I only prayed for you to be happy, as happy as I have been living here."

We sat there on the front porch holding hands and bonding for the first time. I had a lot of questions about my mama and where she been living, but for now, I had no energy to ask them. Orange always said not to rush the big things, and I figured there would be time enough to ask them later. Although I rarely napped during the day, except for when I was sick, I surely felt the need to take one now. Mattie noticed how drained I looked and said, "Child, you should lay down for a spell. Me and your mama will be fine and we'll be here when you wake."

I got up and slowly made my way to the screen door. It was then that I heard it, and my life changed again for the second time that day.

A baby crying.

I turned my head to see the look on Mattie's face, and she was as stunned as I was. Mama nervously looked at both of us as she made her way down the porch steps. Mattie and me followed, and as I neared the automobile, I saw a little baby sleeping in the back seat. I felt a rush of memories come flooding back and I gripped the side of the car to keep from fainting. I saw myself in the back seat, crying out for love, just as this baby was doing.

Mama opened the door and picked up the baby saying, "Child, this here is your baby brother, John Jack."

I had a brother? My whole life changed in that one instant, and as I tried to gather any real thoughts, I reached out to the baby, aching to hold him. Everyone around me disappeared as I took John Jack in my arms, looking at his face for the first time. Time stood still as I held him, and although he had been crying fiercely a minute ago, he now settled down and just stared at me with those big brown eyes. Mattie came to my side and gazed upon the baby for the first time. She said, "Child, he is the spitting image of you, I must say."

"He's beautiful!"

Orange, watching everything from the barn, came over now and when he saw the baby, he said, "Lord have mercy. He is a handsome boy, that's for sure."

Although I had been exhausted minutes before I knew I had a brother, I now felt like I could stay awake for days. I never imagined in all my life that I would have a brother, and now that I did, I didn't want to let him go.

Mama then said, "I didn't know how to tell you about John Jack, but I guess he decided to tell you his self."

Mattie sensed the awkwardness hanging in the air and politely said to Mama, "We best get the baby out of the sun ... "

"I reckon you're right," said Mama.

Taking charge, Mattie then said, "Orange, can you find the Child's old crib in the barn?"

"Yes, Miss Mattie, I'll bring it right over."

Mama then reached out for John Jack, and although I didn't want to give him back, I surely couldn't deny her. She was his mama after all. Mattie, sensing my hesitation, asked me to help Orange in getting the crib down and cleaned up while she and Mama went inside.

I reluctantly put John Jack in Mama's arms and numbly walked to the barn, shocked by all the day's events. Orange was up in the loft looking for the crib, and I just sat down and cried my heart out. I cried for the upset in my life; I cried worried that Mama had come to take me away; and I cried for John Jack, knowing firsthand his life had already not been easy. Orange came down with the crib and asked what he could do to help me with my worries.

I told him Mama had to come to this mountain to find forgiveness, but now her burden had been given to me to carry and I didn't know if I could. No matter how I looked at it, I was going to lose. Either she was going to take me from the only family I ever had, or she would leave, taking John Jack with her, and I would never see him again.

"Hush, Child, hush. Don't you worry 'bout a thing. Orange is here and I won't let nobody take you away."

I swear, for the first time ever, I looked at Orange and saw his eyes wet with tears. I knew he was fretting about today too, and I added his worries to my list of things that made me cry. We worked silently together, fixing up my old crib, and before long it was time to start supper. Orange and me carried the crib to the house and put it in the front room. Mattie, Mama, and John Jack were in the kitchen and I stood by the door watching them, feeling my world had changed in just one day.

Mattie made a real fine supper that night, and I had no hunger for any of it. My plate sat untouched, and even my favorite dessert of blackberry pie couldn't wake me from my fog. After cleaning up from supper, Mattie said Mama and John Jack were going to stay for a few days. I asked Mattie where they was going to sleep, and Mattie said they would stay in the other room downstairs.

So, we spent the rest of the evening cleaning the room and I put a quilt on Mama's bed. Mattie and me hauled in the crib and tucked John Jack in for the night with my old baby quilt. He fell asleep right quick, and I stood there for a few minutes looking at my brother. His hair was darker than mine, but there was no denying our blood relations. I carefully uncoiled his hand from my finger and quietly snuck out of the room.

I joined Mattie and Mama by the roaring fire. The long day had taken a toll on Mama, and within minutes she fell asleep, warmed by the fire at her feet. Mattie knitted while I read a book, and I couldn't help taking sneak peeks at my mama while she slept. I felt funny doing it, but it's like I could see my mama for what she was instead of what she was pretending to be when awake. Her tight jaw was now relaxed and her face seemed softer against the light of the fire. Mattie was right about my mama being pretty. Though it had been many years since I saw her, she still looked young. Her slender frame looked more like a child's than a grown woman's, and her perfectly styled hair was smooth and shiny from the constant brushing. Mama's skin looked flawless, and her hands were smooth. If I hadn't known better, I would have thought she was a city girl. She sure didn't look like she come from the mountain.

I turned to Mattie to find her looking right at me and I smiled shyly, knowing she saw me gazing at Mama. After a few minutes, I said just above a whisper, "Mattie, do you think them bruises is why Mama left and came here?"

"Could be, Child…she got into a tussle with someone I reckon…"

Setting aside my book, I snuggled closer to Mattie, thinking that there was a lot more going on than I understood.

What I failed to notice on Mattie's face was that her pretend smile was hiding deep worries.

Once in bed, I felt the full extent of my exhaustion and fell asleep right away.

The next morning, Orange and I worked on our chores while Mattie started breakfast. Mama and John Jack were still sleeping as I watched the sun rise over the mountains. It wasn't 'til late morning before Mama finally woke. I figured she must have been dog tired and needed a good night's sleep. Mattie said we should head to town today and get some supplies. I offered to go with her and asked Mama if she wanted to come along. Mama said she had come through town on her way up to see us and she had created quite the stir. She thought it would be best if she stayed behind this time and took care of John Jack.

I reckoned Mama had no desire to see the town folk who talked about her all these years. So, Orange continued with chores while Mattie and me loaded the truck and headed down the mountain to trade with old lady Jenkins. Mattie seemed quiet, and though I didn't want to bother her with my thoughts, I just couldn't help myself.

"Mattie, how old you figure John Jack is?"

"I'd figure around eight, maybe ten months old."

"Did Mama say where she been living?"

"No, but I figure it's at least a few days' time from here. I noticed her shoes had red dirt on them. That means she come from the south somewhere."

"Mattie, you think Mama will stay longer than a few days?"

"That's up to her, Child. She is welcome here as long as she wants."

I thought on this for the rest of the drive into town. I knew Mattie would never turn Mama away, especially with a baby, but I didn't think she would need to neither. I thought Mama had a restless spirit 'bout her, and it wouldn't take much time before

Mama felt the need to move on. I just prayed that she didn't want to take me with her. I also prayed I wouldn't have to choose between Mattie and John Jack.

Once in town, Mattie went into the general store to see to her business while I waited in the truck. I sure didn't want to hear the old men talking 'bout my mama today as I had enough things to think about. Within minutes, Bobby Joe come down the main street and headed straight for me.

"How you faring, Child?"

"Fine, thank you."

"I hear your mama is back in town with a young'n. She gonna stay for a while?"

"Not sure about that."

"You be sure to let me know if you be needing anything."

"Yes, sir, Bobby Joe. I sure will."

Just then, Mattie walked out and Bobby Joe tipped his hat to her and quickly ran to her side to help with the supplies. Mattie seemed irritated with his kindness and brushed him off with her hand, but I thought I noticed a slight tint of red rise in her cheeks as if she was blushing from the attention.

As we drove back up the mountain, we both sat silently, absorbed in our own thoughts. Mattie pulled up to the barn and I saw Mama and John Jack relaxing on the front porch. Mama was brushing her hair with a faraway look on her face. It took her a minute to even realize we had come up the road. Once again, I felt funny watching her, as if I had caught a moment of her being herself.

She quickly walked down the steps with John Jack slung on her right hip. As I started unloading the crates, Mattie said, "Why don't y'all take a walk around the mountain?"

"That sounds real nice…" said Mama, and I agreed.

Mama then handed over John Jack and we headed out, taking the windy path down the mountain. I loved exploring and always looked for rocks or treasures to put in my special tin box. Mama had on dress shoes, which made walking these bumpy trails harder. I thought instead I would show her my special spot where I came to think on things. It was a small clearing in the trees and there was a large downed log, perfect for resting on. The forest was thick around us, but the sun always found its way in.

Awhile back, Orange and me cut some strips of tin and hung them from the trees. They tingled in the slight breeze, and when the sun caught them, they'd blind you with their brilliance. Orange once told me you don't have to have money to make your life beautiful, and he sure was right about that. Mama thought my special place was beautiful too. She said when she was just a child, she also had a secret place where she ran to when her papa was being mean, but it wasn't as pretty as mine.

I was sorry to hear about Mama running from her own kin folk, and we sat there for a bit before I said, "Orange once told me kin don't need to be blood."

Mama said, "He sure was right about that, Child. My kin folk was nothing but trouble, and I'm glad to be done with them."

Mama sat there fussing with her dress, her mind drifting back in time to when she lived 'round these parts. I watched her struggle with her memories, holding back anger and fear all at the same time. We sat for quite a spell before I noticed the sun shifting away from us. The day was getting late, and I said we best head back home and help Mattie with supper and chores. Mama just nodded, as she tried to regain her hold on the here and now.

As I got up to leave, I noticed a green stone peeking out from the hollow end of the log. I picked it up and saw it was somewhat translucent, with smooth edges worn by time. It fit perfectly in the palm of my hand and I spit on it, rubbing the dirt off. The rock came to life and the green coloring intensified, glowing like a natural ember. I quickly put the stone in my pocket, feeling I had found my treasure that would represent Mama's and John Jack's coming. We walked back up the path, and I kept thinking of my find and how I couldn't wait to show Orange.

That evening was so nice we decided to eat supper on the front porch. Afterward, Mattie and Mama cleaned up while I sat John Jack on my lap and talked with Orange about my treasure. I carefully took the stone from my pocket and gave it to Orange. After looking at the color of the stone, he then gently held the stone to his eye for a couple of minutes before saying, "You know what you got here?"

"No, what?"

"Child, this here is an emerald. A mighty precious stone- Lord knows it's a big one too."

"You mean I found something valuable?"

"Yes, Child, yes … The emerald is a healing stone. It's good for curing all kinds of ailments. Some folks say if you sleep with the emerald under your pillow, you will be blessed with dreams about the future."

"Do you believe that, Orange?"

"I reckon it's possible. My mama used to call them emerald dreams."

"Emerald dreams, huh?"

"Yep, just keep your stone safe somewheres and don't say nothing to nobody 'bout it."

"I'll put it in my tin and I swear I won't say a thing."

That evening, after Mattie put down John Jack for the night, I watched her knitting by the fire and thought I noticed something different about her face. I tried to figure out what was wrong, but I couldn't put my finger on it. Mama also seemed a little different that night, and every once in a while she would go to the window and look out, as if she was expecting company. Sensing something was wrong, Mattie silently motioned me, turning her head toward the kitchen as she got up and said, "Viola, I'm going to make some hot tea, would you like some too?"

"That sounds nice. Thank you," Mama said.

"I'll help," I said as I quickly followed Mattie into the kitchen.

Mattie whispered to me to go get Orange and close the gate.

"Hurry, Child, and be quiet about it. Use the back door."

"Is something wrong Mattie?"

"I don't know, Child, but I don't want no folks coming up the mountain past dark …"

"Now hurry along, Child," she said as she pushed me out the screen door.

I quickly left and as I walked to Orange's shed, I finally realized what was different about Mattie's face. It was worry. Her face was tighter than it normally looked, as if the worries were pulling at her skin. I never really saw Mattie tense about things, and that's why it took me longer to figure it out.

I knocked at the shed door and Orange called out, "Who's out there?"

"It's me, Orange. Mattie's got some worries."

Orange opened the door and asked, "What's wrong, Child?"

"I ain't sure, to tell you the truth, but Mattie wants us to pull the gate closed and be quick about it."

"Lord have mercy. Let me put my boots on right quick."

Orange laced his boots, grabbed his shotgun, and we headed down the road with a lantern to light the way. The dogs wanted to follow, but Orange gave Pudro the sign to stay put.

I whispered to Orange, "What you think Mattie is worried about?"

"I reckon it has something to do with your mama, Child."

"I sure do hope Mama ain't in some kind of trouble."

"I know, Child, I know. Wait up tonight 'til your Mama goes to bed and then tell Miss Mattie that I'll be sleeping with my boots on and I won't have me no fire neither."

"You'll be cold, Orange."

"Don't you worry 'bout 'ole Orange. I'll be fine, that's for sure."

We pulled the gate closed and quickly walked back.

I ran back to the house, now worried about Orange being cold and how stiff his leg would be in the morning.

I quietly snuck back in through the porch door, and as I sat down, I locked eyes with Mattie. No words were needed.

Sadly, Mama never even noticed I had been gone.

We all stayed up a while longer 'til Mama said she was tired and going to bed.

"Night, Mama," I said.

"Night, Child," she said, and gave me a kiss on my forehead.

Mattie and me waited a few minutes before speaking and then I told Mattie what Orange said.

"Good, Child. Good."

"You think Mama brought us some kind of trouble?"

"I hope not, Child."

We sat together in front of the fire. Mattie went back to her knitting and I thought about Mama. I remember a long time ago, Mattie told me everyone was flawed in one way or another. Some folks work through it and some don't. I couldn't help but think Mama would never get past her troubled childhood. She never did have the right kind of love in her life. Sadly, now she had John Jack to care for, and this worried me to no end. *Could she love the right way the second time around? Had she learned from her mistakes and put her ghosts to rest? I wasn't so sure ...*

What I did know was that the day had worn me out with too many worries, and after a while, my eyes were so heavy I couldn't keep them open any longer.

Mattie said, "You best go to bed, Child. You're falling asleep right here."

"What about you, Mattie?"

"Don't worry 'bout me ... "

Being I was too tired to argue, I said goodnight and happily went upstairs.

Once in bed, I curled up under a layer of quilts and listened carefully for any noise outside. Hearing nothing but the wind and the usual creaks to the house, I quickly fell asleep and had dreams that left me feeling confused.

In one dream, I was fishing in our pond at night. *I caught a big trout, but I could barely see it as the moonlight was covered in a haze of clouds drifting by.*

I struggled to keep hold of the fish, but it wriggled out of my hands and I heard a splash as its belly hit the water. The fish took its life back, swimming away from me until it disappeared in the dark waters. I sat by the pond's edge, looking at my reflection in the water dimly lit by the moon's glow. My face seemed to change with every small ripple that passed over the water, and the second I thought I saw myself, I was gone.

I woke that morning with my dreams still fresh on my mind, knowing that they were trying to tell me something, but I wasn't sure what. I couldn't help but think I had just had my first emerald dream…

Once downstairs, I found Mattie busy in the kitchen while Mama and John Jack were still fast asleep.

"Mattie, did we have any troubles last night?"

"No, Child. I stayed up late with only the fire to keep me company, and all was quiet. Why don't you and Orange open the gate first thing this morning?"

"I'll go find Orange right now."

I walked out on the front porch to see Orange waiting for me. It was still a little dark out, but the sun would be rising soon enough.

"Morning, Orange."

"Morning, Child. How'd ya sleep?"

"Good. Was you cold last night?"

"No, Child, no. I slept like a baby."

I had the feeling this wasn't true as he cupped his hands around the cup of coffee, taking in the warmth he desperately lacked during the night.

"Mattie wants us to open the gate," I said.

Orange took the last sip of his coffee and said, "Miss Mattie is right. We best do that right away."

As we walked down to the bend in the road, I noticed Orange's leg was stiff and he was raising his hip on one side to help pull his leg along. I didn't say nothing 'bout it to Orange, but I felt mad at Mama for him having to sleep without a fire. When we got to the gate, we noticed tire tracks that came right up to the gate and stopped.

Orange carefully looked at the tracks before he said, "Someone must have come up here late last night."

Stunned, I just stood there staring at those tracks knowing this was about mama. After a few minutes, Orange drew a large breath before he said "Child, we gots to tell Miss Mattie 'bout this. This ain't good … ain't good at all."

We quickly pulled open the gate and headed back up. Then I knew I was mad at Mama. Someone came looking for her last night. If Mattie hadn't wanted the gate closed, they might have come all the way up to the mountain.

As we rounded the bend, we saw Mattie waiting for us on the front porch with breakfast. We told her what me and Orange found on the road. After some thinking on the subject, Mattie finally said with a worried look on her face, "Ain't no good news ever come late at night. This is troubling. We can't be having no worries with a baby staying here. We got to be better prepared tonight. Orange, you know what to do, and Child, let's get your mama's automobile in the barn and out of sight."

"Yes, Miss Mattie," said Orange. "Don't you worry 'bout a thing. We'll take care of everything."

The sun hadn't been up long when Mama joined us on the porch. Mattie told her we had a caller late last night and asked if she knew anyone who would come looking for her.

Mama said she left a man behind, but she didn't think he would be able to find her.

"He ain't real bright and he ain't John Jack's daddy," she said. "So, I figured when he finally woke from his drunken sleep and found me and the baby gone, he wouldn't care."

"Well, it looks like someone cares. Is he the one who gave you them bruises?" Mattie asked.

While Mama hesitated answering, I found myself holding my breath, not wanting to hear what she had to say. "Well, about a week ago, things got a little complicated. It was just an accident, but I had John jack's welfare to think about," Mama said.

Although her words were reassuring, her actions told another story. She was slightly shaking and paced back and forth on the porch. Just then, John Jack started crying, so Mama quickly left to feed him.

We all sat there knowing the truth was lying somewhere between what she actually said and what she didn't say. Either way, it wasn't good.

The day passed quickly as we all worked hard to protect the property. I took our truck out of the barn and parked Mama's automobile inside instead. Orange hung tin cans on a string across the path leading up to the house. If anyone decided to come on foot, the cans would alert us.

Of course, we didn't want to forget about the dogs. They didn't take kindly to folks coming 'round that they didn't know. They would surely wake us with their barking if someone got close to the house.

Later that afternoon, I sat down with Mama on the porch and played with John Jack. He was sitting on my lap and I was making funny faces at him, which he seemed to like. John Jack was such a calm baby and rarely fussed. Mama watched us together, and I could tell how much she was enjoying herself.

I had been dreading talking to her about her plans, as I feared what she was going to say. My worries were getting the best of me though, and I needed to know.

"Mama, how long you think you going to stay here on the mountain?"

"Not sure 'bout that, Child. I was thinking 'bout heading out west and looking for work. Folks say it's real pretty, and maybe I could start a new life with John Jack. I would like you to come with us and we could all be a family."

My fears came to life right then. I knew in my heart of hearts that's why Mama came here. She wanted to claim me after all these years. I tried to collect my thoughts, but the pounding inside my head kept me from getting a grasp on them. The way I saw it, either I had to abandon John Jack just as I was starting to bond with him, or I had to forsake the only family I had ever known. My heart raced as I tried to choose my words carefully.

"Mama, I have a family here. I love you, but living on this here mountain with Mattie and Orange has been my life. I belong here. I am so grateful you came back, and God knows I already care for John Jack, but I love Mattie and Orange."

Mama said nothing as she rocked in the chair. Finally, with a great weariness to her voice, she said, "Child, I want my children together … with me."

"If you really loved me, you wouldn't be putting your own wishes above mine. You brought me here years ago for a reason. You knew I would be happy. Now you want to take that all away from me … because you changed your mind?"

I watched Mama holding back tears and I knew she was trying to make things right in her life. But for me, it was too late. She had her chance when I was a baby and she couldn't do it. Just then, I thought about my dream and I finally understood the meaning. *I was the fish taking back its life!* It wasn't me at the pond fishing, it was Mama. That's why my reflection was confusing.

I looked Mama right in the eyes and, "Mama, you can't take me away from Mattie and Orange … they need me and I need them. This is my home. The way I see things is if you want a family, then you best do right by John Jack."

There, I'd said it. I'd made up my mind and said my piece. It was up to Mama now on what to do.

I stood up and handed John Jack back to Mama, her eyes pleading with me to stay as she wiped away her tears.

As I walked away from Mama, I heard her calling out to me, "I'm trying to do right by you, Child. I'm trying—"

Her words fell on deaf ears.

I found Orange in the barn. He took one look at me and asked, "What's wrong, Child?"

"I took my life back today," I said.

The night was quiet, as everyone had a lot on their minds. Mattie looked worried and I figured it might be because she feared someone from Mama's past might come callin' again.

Earlier in the day, when I took my life back, it freed me in some way. It was like I always knew that Mama would come one day, and now that she had, I could put that worry to rest. Mama, on the other hand, seemed hurt and was clinging to John Jack like he was her only salvation. She fussed over him all night before she finally put him down to sleep.

After a while, I looked over to Mattie to find she had nodded off. Staying up late the night before had caught up with her, but I didn't feel funny watching her sleep like I did with Mama. I pulled the quilt up over her shoulders, knowing I would stay up late so she could rest.

Mama seemed to be deep in her thoughts as she stared into the fire. Before long, she said she should retire to bed. As mama bent down to kiss me good-night, I noticed a trace of dried tears on her face, and I selfishly pretended like I didn't see it.

I must have stayed up for a couple more hours without one real thought in my head. I was tired from all the thinking the past few days, and I just wanted things to be easy again. Mattie finally woke and thanked me for letting her sleep. As I got up and walked toward the stairs, Mattie reached for my hand and said, "Child, I won't let your mama take you away. I heard what she said to you this afternoon on the porch. I was proud of you. You said what was in your heart."

"It's in God's hands now, Mattie. Ain't nothing more we can do."

I woke to birds singing in the trees. I laid there for a few minutes enjoying the harmony of the morning, not wanting to get out of bed. I opened my window to see the sun just peeking over the mountaintop. It was beautiful and I appreciated the sun showing off like it did. I quickly dressed and went down stairs to see Mattie in the kitchen. I called out to her as I went out the front door, saying I would get with Orange and open the gate.

I found Orange and we started down the road. As we rounded the bend, I saw the gate was already open.

"Did you open the gate, Orange?" I asked nervously, already knowing the answer.

"No, Child no … something is wrong. We best get Miss Mattie," he said.

Something was wrong all right … I should have known it the minute I woke up. Things seemed too calm this morning and nothing about the last few days had been peaceful. I left Orange at the top of the road as I ran to the house.

"Mattie!" I called out as I swung open the porch screen. "The gate is already open. What happened last night after we went to bed? Did someone come calling?"

Mattie never took her eyes off the dough she was kneading. She nervously said, "Child, I heard your mama leave late last night."

"What? What do you mean? She changed her mind and left me here? Oh Lord, she took John Jack. I didn't even get to say goodbye to him."

Sadly, the thought of Mama being gone gave me a sigh of relief wrapped in guilt; however, the thought of not seeing John Jack again made me weak in the knees.

Mattie came to me and let me cry while she held me tight.

"Child, I'm sorry you're sad. I know how much you cared for John Jack. I also know your mama will take good care of him. She loves that boy."

"Mattie, I told her yesterday how much I needed you and Orange. I never gave thought to how much she needed me, though. Now I got to figure out how to forgive myself."

"Don't be so hard on yourself, Child. I reckon she knew from the minute she set foot on this mountain that this was where you belonged."

I wiped my tears on Mattie's apron and said I should let Orange know they were gone. I slowly walked back outside with a light head and a heavy heart.

I found Orange on the porch and I told him that Mama and John Jack were gone. I reckon he already knew when he saw the gate, but he didn't want to tell me.

"Child, I know you is sad about your mama and John Jack, but I want you to know how sad 'ole Orange would have been waking up this beautiful morning and finding you gone too."

I reached for his hand and held it tight. With tears in my eyes and a smile on my face, Orange knew exactly what I was saying. As usual, there was no need for words.

Mattie joined us on the porch and we all sat, trying to rock our fears away. My thoughts wandered back to little John Jack, bouncing in the back seat down a dusty road, all alone. Sadness welled up inside me again, and just as I felt I could not hold back the flood of tears, I heard a cry.

My heart stopped.

I listened for something again, but only heard my heart beating against my chest. Then I heard it again ... *Oh Lord, could it be?*

I ran into the house and flung open the bedroom door to find John Jack in his crib crying. I swept him up in my arms and he settled down right quick and stopped crying. I think he knew he was home, just like I had many years ago.

"Oh, John Jack, I sure is glad to see you!"

I rocked him back and forth and thanked the good Lord above for my blessing. Mattie and Orange stood by the door smiling and I heard Orange say, "Things is going to be just fine 'round here, just fine indeed."

Mattie said today was a day for celebrating. I passed John Jack to Mattie, who kissed on him. Orange then held his arms out and Mattie gave him John Jack, who got showered with love once again.

Just days ago my life was so upside down but that day everything was right were it should be! I thanked God for listening to my prayers and arranging things in a way I didn't even know I needed. I now knew what my purpose was: to take care of John Jack and help Mattie raise him right. This is not to say I didn't have sad feelings about Mama leaving, because I did.

For the second time in Mama's life, she gave a gift of pure love to someone else. I realized now that she was stronger than I thought.

Back on the mountain, we spent the day doting on John Jack. Mattie baked a small cake and we celebrated the day his life began! John Jack seemed to like all the attention, and when it was time for him to take a nap, we sadly let him out of our arms for some well-deserved sleep. I took him to his crib, and as I put the quilt over him, I found a note left from Mama.

Dear Child,

I want you to know how proud I am of you! You have a beautiful life, one that I want John Jack to share. My heart aches for both of you already, but I know it's the right thing to do. Mattie has done a fine job rearing you, and I know John Jack's life will be filled with more love than I ever could provide.

I will write you once I get settled. I know how much you like looking for treasures, so when you find the one I left for you … keep it safe until we see each other again.

Love,
Mama

Months later, we got our first piece of mail at the post office. It was from Mama. She said she had settled out west in a small town, worked in a dress shop, and loved it. She lived above the shop in a small apartment that was across from a park. She ate lunch in the park and her nights were spent sewing or reading.

"I feel like I've come home, Child," she said.

I wrote her back that very night. It was the first letter sent in a long line of letters that I mailed every week and continued to for years. The town Mama settled in had been known for centuries by the local Indians as "The Valley of Peace." I reckoned Mama had finally found her own piece of heaven.

Anyway, not long after Mama left, I walked down to my special place in the woods. I sat there thinking about Mama and prayed she was all right. The wind blew gently, winding its way through my tin strips and distracting me from my thoughts. It was then I saw a note dangling from string. It was from Mama, and it said that to find my treasure, I must look in the dark for the truth. I wondered about this for a while and then it dawned on me. I reached my hand into the hollow log and pulled out a leather-bound book. I opened to the first page to find a sketch of me. It was the first time I saw what I looked like as a baby. Page after page were pencil sketches of me during my first few years. I never even knew Mama liked to draw, and here was proof of her love for me. I could feel it with every page I turned.

A FAMILY
IS BORN ...

John Jack thrived, living with us on the mountain. We doted on him and we all felt like our family was complete. We moved out all of Pappy's boxes and things and put them in the barn loft so John Jack's room was officially his own. Orange fixed an old trunk we found in the barn and I painted John Jack's name on it with a moon and stars. Mattie put some of his quilts and toys inside. I figured as he got older, it would be the perfect place for his treasures. John Jack still slept in his crib when he wasn't curled up in my lap. That boy loved to fall asleep in my arms by the fire. He was a stunning-looking baby, with large brown eyes and dark brown, curly hair. His smile alone could melt your heart, and it was hard not to spoil him every minute of the day.

Soon after Mama left, Bobby Joe came calling on us. I expected his visit, as he seemed to know all that was going on 'round the mountain.

Mattie always acts like he was intruding on our chores, but I think she likes seeing him and just won't admit it to herself.

I brought out John Jack to meet Bobby Joe, who was rocking in the porch chair.

"Bobby Joe, this here is my brother," I said.

"What a handsome-looking boy! He sure do look like you, Child," Bobby Joe said.

"Thank you kindly," I said, beaming.

"Looks like y'all are taking good care of him, that's for sure. Is your mama coming back to live on the mountain?" he asked.

"No, I don't think so."

"I see. Well, I have no doubt you and Mattie will take good care of him."

"Thank you."

"Speaking of Mattie, where is she today?"

"Orange and Mattie should be back any minute. They was down the side of the mountain picking the last of the berries while John Jack napped."

We both sat for a minute, quietly. I was thinking about Bobby Joe liking Mattie, and I reckon Bobby Joe was thinking the same thing.

"Bobby Joe, you should have supper with us tonight," I said. "Mattie makes a mighty fine pie, I must say."

"Thank you. That would be nice."

Just then, Mattie and Orange appeared over the mountaintop and headed our way.

Bobby Joe stood up and tipped his hat politely to Mattie.

"Nice to see you, Mattie," he said.

Mattie nodded and said, "Good to see you, Bobby Joe. What can I do for you today?"

"Not a thing, Mattie, not a thing. I was just looking in on y'all—"

"Mattie, I asked Bobby Joe to join us for supper tonight," I quickly said.

Mattie looked a little flustered, but her voice was steady as she said, "Oh, well that sounds nice. I best get busy then," and went inside.

Supper was interesting, watching Bobby Joe and Mattie. They were both polite to each other while I saw Bobby Joe sneak more than one look toward Mattie. I fed John Jack some mashed potatoes that he then smeared all over his face and we all laughed watching his antics. He was just starting to eat some food other than milk and he seemed to like the attention as much as the food. He had grown a lot the past few months and was starting to babble. Although you couldn't understand any real words, we pretended that we could.

We said goodbye to the summer that changed our lives, and as fall approached, we prepared for the winter months that lay ahead. We could tell that it was going to be a hard winter, as it was already colder than usual for that time of year. Before long, the pond was frozen over and snow blanketed the mountaintop. Our days were spent working in the bitter cold, and come night, we were all exhausted from being out in the snow and wind. John Jack was too little to be outside, so most days, Mattie tended to his needs inside while me and Orange did all the chores.

By nightfall, when I finally came in for the day, John Jack would always smile when he saw me. I loved the fact that he missed me, and I would dote on him until I put him down to sleep. Sitting by the fire with Mattie was always one of my favorite times of the day. We talked about Christmas and what we were going to do to make John Jack's first Christmas on the mountain special. We decided Mattie would make all the food, I would decorate the tree, and Orange would help both of us making gifts.

The next day we set about our chores, and by late afternoon, Orange and me went to the barn to start on Christmas gifts. Orange wanted to make John Jack his own rocking chair for the front porch, and I wanted to make him a stool so he could reach things. John Jack was crawling around the house and I figured he would be walking in no time.

The next few weeks flew by, and before we knew it, it was the night before Christmas. Mattie was busy in the kitchen as Orange and me cut down the Christmas tree and put it in the front room. It was about four feet tall and John Jack loved staring at it. I used fishing line to hang dried berries, painted some pine cones and put them in the branches, and made a star that I put at the top of the tree. It was real pretty and perfect for John Jack's first Christmas.

Mattie told me when I was little that Saint Nick would come down the fireplace and leave a treat for everyone in the house. Although I knew this wasn't true, I still liked believing.

"Miracles happen every day, Child," she'd say. "You just got to open your heart is all." We all sat around the fire that night and drank tea while we admired the tree. We ate cookies that Mattie baked and even John Jack nibbled on some. He was too young to understand what was going on, but we were excited for him. Orange and me put our gifts wrapped in burlap under the tree. Mattie brought out a gift for each of us that she had been working on and we all sat back and admired our treasures. It was a magical night for us as we sat by the fire reminiscing and fussing over John Jack. I truly felt blessed to have such a wonderful family, and I went to bed that night dreaming of stars dancing in the sky.

Christmas morning was full of excitement as we ate breakfast in front of the fire. Mattie made biscuits and gravy for Orange, bacon for me, and coffee for all of us. I helped John Jack open his gift from

Mattie, which was a winter cap and coat that Mattie hand-knitted. It was a perfect fit and Mattie beamed with pride. Orange loved the quilt we made him, and in the corner I stitched his name in the color orange. My gift under the tree was a wooden box to hold all my treasures. It had stars carved on the top and a beautiful iron latch to keep my rocks safe.

Finally, Mattie opened her gift and was surprised to see a store-bought brush and comb set. For the past month, Orange and me secretly traded with old lady Jenkins while Mattie had no idea. It was a set that came with a mirror and would look lovely in her room. Mattie's eyes were wet with tears as she hugged us both and said this was the best Christmas ever.

We had to agree with her … everything felt perfect.

Mattie then brought out a package Mama had sent for John Jack and me through the mail. I opened the gift and I could not believe my eyes! Mama had painted a picture of the park across from her apartment.

Something in the picture spoke to me. The bench was shaded by a large tree with branches drooping ever so graceful. A slight breeze moved through the tree and the leaves seemed to dance right off the canvas. The fountain sprayed a fine mist into the air, blurring the sun's heat while a lone bird sat perched enjoying a midday bath.

The coloring of the picture was soft and the brushstrokes were confident and sure. I could feel the changes in Mama just by looking at the picture, and my heart ached with happiness. It was my first glimpse into her new life, and it all felt right. Mama really did it; she finally fit into her world.

John Jack was too little to appreciate the painting or the gifts Orange and me made him, but we knew he would love them as he got older.

I hung Mama's picture over the fireplace. It seemed fitting to see it in such a central part of the room. Orange was reading to John Jack as Mattie worked in the kitchen preparing for an early supper. I happily just sat back and took it all in. The aromas coming from the kitchen, the fresh pine smell of our tree, and the painting so beautifully displayed. It really was the best Christmas!

That winter had been harsh, and I had never been so thankful to see the snow melt and the days getting warmer. With springtime right on our heels, we were all happy to be outside and working together again. John Jack was taking small steps and hanging onto everything he could find. He was adorable to watch as he tried to keep up with us.

Thankfully, the summer was extra beautiful, as a reward to the hard winter we had endured. John Jack loved being outdoors and I often carried him down the mountain to my special place. He loved to sit and stare at the tin dangling in the tree branches as they made their music in the breeze. He was now talking in one-word sentences, and I smiled as he said over and over again, "Pretties, pretties."

Never a day went by that I didn't thank the good Lord above for my blessings. When I think back to when I was little and living with Mama, if I could have formed the right words, I would have wished for the life I have right now. I know it ain't perfect, nobody's is, but Mattie once told me, "Life is a journey, and sometimes we shine brighter than other times."

"What do you mean?" I asked.

"One day, when you're older you'll understand."

Mattie was right. One night, as I watched the fireflies from the front porch with John Jack, I thought back about what Mattie had said. Sometimes the fireflies dazzled you with their light and other times they flew in darkness. No matter what, they always kept flying. I reckon that's what Mattie was trying to say. You just got to keep trying is all and have faith it will all work out, even when you can't see where you are headed.

That summer was my favorite of all my summers growing up on the mountains. We were all working side by side and the land never looked better. The garden thrived under Mattie's love and attention and we had more food than we could eat. Orange had the house and barn in the best shape they had ever been in and I could tell he took great pride in them. Some nights, I would see him stand back with his thumbs hooked in his overalls, looking over his work with a smile on his face. The barn had become his

space and everything was neatly organized just to
his liking. John Jack spent many an hour out there
with Orange, following him around, pulling on his
overalls, all the while pointing to things and saying,
"What's that? What's that?"

Orange loved teaching him the right words for
things and they never tired of each other. They were
complete opposites who, together, made one whole
piece.

Sometimes I would look at our family and wonder how we all came to find each other. I know the
town folk found us all to be a bit odd, but I didn't
care. For years they talked about Mama behind my
back, and now the main topic was the four of us.

One day, I heard one of the old men say we were
just a bunch of misfits, living God-knows-what kind
of life up there in the mountains. I remembered what
Mattie said 'bout them not having enough love, and
I held onto that thought real hard as they minded
our business.

Seems that time passes quicker when everything is
right in your life. That's how the summer was. The
days were filled with work and tending to John Jack.
He liked working the soil in the garden with Mattie just so he could roll around in the cool dirt. He
seemed to love the mountains and wanted to spend
the better part of the day outside getting into some-

thing. Suppertime was a mix of emotions for him; he so wanted to eat, but did not want to go inside. I usually gave him a bath after dinner and we would sit out on the front porch listening to the critters. Orange would play his harmonica and John Jack would entertain us by jumping around to the music. It was a sight to see and we wondered what we did for fun before he came to live with us.

John Jack seemed to complete all of us. It's like we was just waiting for him to come into our lives without even knowing it.

Time passed quickly as the days turned into months and the months turned into years.

John Jack was truly the light of our lives and our entire world revolved around his needs. As he got older, we found out that boy loved climbing! He would climb the trees so far up it would give us quite the fright. Many times Orange was the only one who could coax him down with his bargaining skills.

Everyone took turns minding John Jack during the day, but for the most part, he loved following Orange around. The mountain was his life, and we loved watching him discover everything for the first time. He seemed to be a fearless boy, but thankfully, he was not reckless. I think he just felt at ease with the outdoors, as he longed to explore and understand every inch of the mountain.

Most days you could find John Jack alongside Orange or fishing in the pond. Oh, how that boy loved to fish! If he wasn't fishing, he was swimming in the pond trying to catch fish bare-handed. More than once, we had to wade into the water to get him out as he didn't want to go in for the night.

We always set aside time after supper for John Jack's studies, and he was becoming quite a good reader. Orange was a natural teacher who had the patience to sit for hours on end and answer all of John Jack's questions. Believe me when I say he wanted to understand everything.

The town folk who would have loved to just sit back and talk about him instead found him captivating. He was an outgoing boy whose good looks charmed both the young and the old. John Jack had a sincere interest in what folks were doing and acted older than he actually was. He didn't have the silly personality that other five-year-old boys did, and he was rarely disciplined by any of us, because most of the time there was no need. His calm, mature nature combined with large brown eyes and beautiful curly locks disarmed even the hardest of the old timers.

Now mind you, they still talked about all of us, but when it came to John Jack, they only had nice things to say.

Mama and me still wrote, and when John Jack was older, he helped me with the letters. He understood, as best as he could, that Mama lived somewhere else, and that was just normal to him. He had a picture of Mama in his room, and unlike me at his age, he had a sense of who she was.

Mama stopped working at the dress shop and started painting for a living. Hard to believe someone could make money from painting, but she did. Turned out, she made a name for herself, and folks bought her paintings from all around the state. Every week when she wrote, she also put money in with the letter. She said she wanted John Jack and me to spend it how we saw fit. I usually gave some to Mattie to help out and the rest I saved. Over the years, the money added up, and I filled more than one coffee can. I reckoned there would come a day when I'd be glad to have it, and until then, it was hidden under my bed for safekeeping.

WINTER'S THAW
RAINS TEARS

Orange had slowed down a bit over time, but he still enjoyed walking in the woods with me and exploring. It was during one of those outings that he told me he hid his special treasures under the 'ole oak tree. I asked him why he went ahead and did such a thing, and he said, "Child, ain't nobody going to go digging 'round no old graves."

I said, "I'm not so sure about that. You did."

Well, he just laughed and laughed. Then I started laughing, and before you know it, I plum forgot about what he said and was just taking in the moment. Orange was like that. He was easygoing, and he had a calmness about him that I found comforting.

I looked up to Orange in a way that only a child can with a parent. His skin might be darker, and he might have missed my younger years, but none of that mattered. We had become an unlikely family, bonded by our friendship and love for one another.

Sadly, as time went on, Orange couldn't walk the steep paths with his sore leg, climb the roof for repairs, or bend down for hours working in the garden. Instead, he spent more time on the front porch reading to John Jack and playing the harmonica. His weary body seemed to be getting smaller and smaller. I never did know how old Orange was when he came to live with us, and God knows we were all aging in our own way, but Orange just seemed to be aging the fastest.

For years, the town folk talked about Orange living with us out on the mountain; how it was improper and we should be ashamed of ourselves. Mattie always said that love comes into your life in many different ways. Orange had been destined to be our good friend and nobody had the right to say otherwise. We made a difference in his life and he made a difference in ours. Mattie trusted her own heart and we were all blessed because of it. I guess it's just another way of how Mattie seemed to care for the ones who needed it most, and in doing so, we all learned a lesson in love.

One day as winter was nearing done, Orange talked about not feeling well. He had been moving slower than usual that day, and I wasn't a bit surprised to hear him say he would be retiring to bed early that evening. When he didn't join us for breakfast, I went out to the shed to check on him. I knew right off something was wrong, as there was no smoke coming from the chimney, even though it was a cold morning. I knocked on the door real gentle-like, and when Orange didn't respond, I slowly opened the shed door, calling out his name.

"Orange?"

When he didn't answer, I walked into the shed and immediately sensed something was wrong. Although everything looked the same, it all felt different. Empty. Moving to his bedside as if I was in a dream, I saw Orange curled up like a small child under his quilt. Slowly, I reached out and touched his hand and a cold shiver ran up my spine. My heart swelled in my chest as I tried to hold back my fear that I knew was true. Orange was gone.

He had passed sometime during the night, and although he looked peaceful, my heart ached for the loss of his friendship already. I sat next to him on the bed and cried and cried with such sorrow that my body felt wracked with pain at a depth unknown to me in the past. The sound of my own moaning was foreign to me, like an animal, and not from a human being. I don't reckon I know how long I sat there, but I know it seemed like forever. My life felt scary for the first time, and I didn't want to leave his side, so I curled up next to Orange and held his hand trying to keep his cold body warm.

"Orange, you can't leave me. You just can't!"

It was then I began pleading with God to make him all better. I knew it was silly and that he was already gone, but I wanted to believe that my love for him could bring him back. Not knowing how to live without Orange, I just laid there with him and waited for the world to stop spinning.

Sometime later I walked back to the main house to fetch Mattie, and my thoughts wandered through time, remembering all the years we shared. I looked back once more at the shed and only saw my trail of hot tears melting in the snow, leaving a path of grief to mark this day.

Mattie, me, and John Jack buried Orange alongside her mama and sister. She said it was the right thing to do. He might not have been blood kin, but he was kin in our hearts. We had to ask Bobby Joe for his help in digging the grave, as the ground was still hard from the winter months. It was a painful time for us, and my heart broke into pieces as we laid him in the ground. I told Mattie I couldn't bear the thought of Orange being cold, so she tucked him in one of his quilts before closing the wood coffin lid. I did however, keep the quilt we made him years before with his name on it, and I laid it at the foot of my bed where it stayed for years to come. Every night I held the quilt close to my face, breathing in Orange's scent, and just for that moment, I felt whole again.

That morning, as the new day's light rose over the mountaintop, my life as I knew it was over.

I made a beautiful cross to mark his grave. It had the heart-shaped stone that I found the first week Orange came to live with us. I tied leather laces around it and put it at the top of the cross. I painted his name in the middle and John Jack put stars on either side. Mattie said it was mighty pretty and knew Orange would have loved it.

I could barely see what I was doing as I dug a hole for the cross. Tears pooled in my eyes and dropped to the ground, polluting the soil with my sorrow. I worked mindlessly, digging deeper and deeper until my shovel hit something hard in the dirt. My fingers groped in the cool soil, expecting to pull out a rock, and instead I found myself pulling out a tin box.

I suddenly remembered Orange telling me about hiding his treasures under the oak tree. I held it in my hands not knowing what to do. This seemed so personal, yet Orange would have never told me about it if he didn't want me to find it. I held the tin close to me and I cried for all the new memories we would not be making together.

That evening, Mattie and me sat by the fire staring at the tin … It's like we was waiting for some kind of sign, and when one didn't come, we waited some more. Finally, I told Mattie we were being silly. The message we were waiting for was the one Orange gave me long ago by telling me about the tin. With shaking hands, I lifted the lid and shyly peered inside.

The first thing I saw was a picture of a baby. A baby!

"Mattie, it's a baby!"

We both stared at the photo of a little girl, maybe around one year old. She was wearing a white dress, matching bonnet, and had black locks of hair peeking out around her ears. She was a beautiful child, and as I stared into her dark eyes, my mind raced with questions. *Who was she?* I handed the photo to Mattie as I looked back in the tin for answers. I found a letter written so long ago the words were faded and the paper felt fragile in my hands. I carefully unfolded the paper and read aloud to Mattie.

Dearest Orange,

You must know how it pained me to leave you behind without so much as a word. Mama found out my sin, and although I never told anyone about you, I knew you would not be safe if we

were found out. Please understand I left to protect you, and not a day goes by that I don't think
about you. Maybe in a different time our love
would be enough, but sadly it was not meant to
be in our lifetime.

If given any chance to come back to the mountain, I will find you.

All my love,
Alexandra

Mattie and me just stared at the letter like it had
been written in another language. My hands were
slightly trembling as I set the letter down and said,
"Orange had a secret love!"

I always wondered why Orange did not have a
family, and now we knew. He found his one true love,
and I reckon he waited for her, hoping she would
come back to the mountains again. Was the picture
of the little baby his baby girl? I turned the picture
over for clues and all I saw was a name: Abby Mae.

"Mattie, do you think Abby Mae is Orange's
baby?"

"I ain't sure, Child. I reckon it's possible."

"I pray she's his baby!"

I liked the thought that there could be a part
of Orange still alive. I looked closer at the picture,
studying her eyes and chin, hoping that something
would stand out that reminded me of Orange. Other
than her dark hair and eyes, all I saw was a pretty
little girl. I don't know what I expected to find in the
tin, but this wasn't it.

I put the picture with the letter aside and looked in the tin. Once again, it was not what I expected. Inside was a key with a note attached.

The note said:

> Be still your thoughts, Child,
> and listen to the music.
> Hidden for years past
> Where thoughts are lulled
> Is a treasure unlike any other.

Mattie stared at me as I held the key.

"Mattie, what does all this mean?"

"I reckon I don't know. Everything in this tin has me guessing. I think we best sleep on it and maybe in the morning our thoughts will be clearer."

Exhausted, I curled up to Mattie just like I did when I was little and I told her my troubles. "I don't want any of these things, Mattie. I want Orange back. If I knew he was sick and nearing the end of his life, I would have given everything I owned to keep him here with us for just even one more day!"

Mattie stroked my hair, trying to calm me down, and said it don't work that way. "When the good Lord says it's your time, it's your time. It ain't anything we can control, Child. We had a good many years together and we got to be thankful for that."

I knew what Mattie was saying to be true. I just didn't like it.

That night I dreamed I was sitting at the mountain's edge, peering into the thick dense fog that hovered over the valley below. *The night surrendered itself to ominous black clouds that moved across the sky, darkening the glow of the full moon. Dangling my legs over the mountaintop, I reached down to feel the thick fog when I heard a wolf howl. The eerie moans traveled deep from within the dense forest, and as they got closer, the moans got louder and louder, searching ...*

Quickly, I got up and ran as fast as I could toward the house as the moans closed in on me, and just as I shut the screen door, the moans stopped. Standing safely inside the house, I looked out into the darkness and saw two glowing eyes peering back at me. The wolf had been searching all right ... for me.

I woke the next morning thinking about my dream. I was used to giving extra thoughts to my nighttime adventures, as they seemed to be a window into what was happening in my life. I curled up in Orange's quilt and reached for my special box. Carefully opening the latch, I held the emerald stone that only Orange and me knew about. I rubbed the stone as I thought about my dream, wondering why that wolf wanted me. I was confused by its meaning, just as I felt confused with my life right now.

John Jack was also having a really hard time with Orange's death, in part because he was too young to fully understand why his friend was gone. We explained to him that Orange went home to be with God, but John Jack just kept saying that Orange's home was here.

I knew exactly how he felt. We all felt cheated, and there wasn't a darn thing we could do about it.

That evening, I finally put my thoughts down on paper and wrote Mama the sad news. I told her our hearts were aching something fierce, and we was trying to find some kind of comfort in our new life. I let her know we were faring the best we could under the circumstances.

What I didn't say was how I felt like I was one big open wound. My emotions were just barely hidden under the skin, raw and unpredictable. I felt at any moment I would collapse from the heartache I was feeling, never to be whole again. I didn't tell Mama any of this, as I didn't want to scare her the way I was scaring myself.

I don't know if it was wishful thinking or I was just noticing for the first time, but John Jack seemed to have some of Orange's mannerisms. I took note of the way he hooked his little hands in his overalls, and the way he walked with a purpose but like he had all the time in the world. Mostly, I took note of his calm personality. Maybe I needed to see these things or maybe it was real. I wasn't sure to tell you the truth.

It wasn't 'til a while later, when I finally had the heart to enter the shed that I found writings from Orange addressed to us. He must have felt his time was coming, as the letter was dated weeks before his death. Mattie says humans have an instinct just like animals about dying. She said it's a private affair between you and the Lord, and during this time, many confess their sins and pray to the Lord above for redemption and a quick passage.

Carefully breaking the seal, I unfolded the paper and looked upon Orange's written words:

Dear Family,

I hereby leaves all my goods to Miss Mattie, the Child, and John Jack.

I reckon the good Lord has other plans for me, so don't you worry 'bout it none.

Child, I am the owl that keeps the night safe and the mountain soil that sweetens the corn.

> I swears,
> Orange

That was just the first surprise I found that day in Orange's shed. I took a moment to think about the will and all that he wrote. I liked the idea of Orange watching out for us, and I believed every word of it. All the years before he came to live with us, I never knew what I missed by not having a father around. I knew now. For the first time since Orange passed, I was grateful for the pain in my heart. Without that pain, I would have never known the man I would forever consider my papa.

I sadly gathered up Orange's belongings, just as I had done with Pappy's many years before, and I took them into the house. I showed Mattie the will, and she sat down in front of the fire and read and re-read the official paper. I knew she was struggling with her own memories, and I didn't want to disturb her thoughts.

I brewed some fresh coffee and sat at the kitchen table to look through some of the goods Orange had left us. As I dug through the first crate, I found exactly what I expected. Pots and pans he sold on the road, beads for making jewelry, books for the young kids, maps, seeds, and all kinds of small toys and tools. It wasn't until I went through the third crate that I found a leather-bound book tied with a leather strap to keep it closed. In it were the records from all the sales he made over the years. It showed what folks traded to him or what he sold and the money collected. Over the years, Orange did a lot of traveling throughout the state, and there were folks listed by name I did not recognize.

Some folks in the poorest regions of the area owed him money, and it showed a due balance in the book. Mattie then came in and sat with me, pouring herself a cup of coffee and reflecting on the day's discoveries. She said Orange told her once that the people in most need of his goods had no money. He would often trade for things he had no need for or sell something real cheap, saying he needed to be rid of it to bring in new goods. Of course, none of this was exactly true.

Come to find out, all them years we traded fresh eggs and corn with him, he actually was giving them to a family across the valley that was in desperate need. He told Mattie they had three kids and the mother looked very thin, trying to provide for the little ones first.

Although I understood how troubling the times had been for so many folks, I was sheltered from that knowledge when I was younger. Mattie said a child need not be worrying about such things. We closed the book and put it back in the crate, knowing we would never collect any unpaid monies from anyone. Orange would have wanted it that way.

As I watched John Jack playing on the kitchen floor with one of the toys, I thought about the other mountain folks being in far more need than we were, like the family Orange helped out. We were not rich folks by any means, but we never went without a meal or a warm fire to sit by.

"Mattie, you think we could give some of these things Orange left us to that woman with three kids?"

"Child, that's a great idea! Orange would love it!"

So, we set aside some of the goods from the crates for the family we were soon to help. We retired that evening feeling emotionally spent but looking forward to our first trip to the other side of the valley.

We quietly gathered some extra supplies over the next few weeks to take with us. Times were still hard for most folks, and we didn't want to draw attention to our efforts. By the end of the month, we felt like we had enough supplies to plan our trip the following day. Mattie used Orange's ledger book for directions, and we had the name of the mother, Shelby, who we were going to call on. We loaded the truck and parked it safely in the barn for the night. All we had to do in the morning was gather a few more fresh eggs, have breakfast, and be on our way.

We set out early, just as the sun was rising over the mountaintop. It was going to be a beautiful clear morning, cold but clear. The truck was heavy with the goods in the back, which helped to navigate the windy roads down the mountain. We really had no idea how long the trip would take, as that was the first time we had taken a drive to the other side of the valley. Mattie brought her trusty shotgun, as expected, and we also put Pudro in the back of the truck where I had made a small bed area behind the crates to keep him out of the cold wind. John Jack wanted to ride in the back with the dog, but Mattie flatly refused, saying it was too cold. John Jack spent the morning sitting on my lap, and after a while, he settled down and fell asleep.

Normally, I would be lulled by the engine and my mind would wander back to the days when I was little and with Mama. However, I felt like I had put those ghosts to rest, and as I looked at John Jack sleeping, I remembered that Mattie said God had a plan for all of us. I think Mattie's calling was to take care of me and Orange. In turn, I was to take this blessing and care for John Jack.

My memories of my life with Mama faded little by little with each passing year, and I think it was a sign that I should keep focused on my calling, which was John Jack.

As we rounded the hills on the other side of the mountains, I looked around at the new terrain and noticed small houses tucked back into the woods. Smoke was curling out of the chimneys, and dogs barked as they followed the truck lumbering slowly down the road. The truck squeaked every time we hit a small bump in the road, which was many, and before long, John Jack woke and barked back at the dogs hounding us.

We turned up a road that was marked "Private/ No Trespassing" that Mattie believed to be the house we were looking for. I just hoped we would be welcome, as some folks don't take kindly to strangers callin'. We took the road slow and easy, as to make our appearance known as friendly. We wasn't even parked yet and their dogs had already surrounded the truck. Two dogs jumped on the doors, scratching the metal with their nails, causing Pudro to growl at them, flashing his yellow teeth.

Within minutes, a slight woman came out and stood on the porch staring at the situation before she would come closer. When she saw us in the truck, she called off the dogs and they obediently ran to the front porch and stood by her side. Mattie then unrolled the window and said loudly, "My name is Mattie. I come from the other side of the mountain to see you. I am a friend of Orange's … "

This put the woman more at ease, and she motioned for us to come her way.

Mattie got out of the truck, grabbing Pudro, and putting him in the front cab while I carried John Jack. We walked to the front porch and the woman took one look at us and figured we were her kind, and she invited us in for a cup of hot tea. The house was cold and dusty, with loose floorboards in desperate need of repair. The walls were bare, except for a cross and a couple of old pictures hanging over the fireplace. Sadly, the house had no life to it and stood as just a roof over someone's head instead of a home. Our home always had a lingering aroma of food, but this house had none.

Once settled in the kitchen, the woman set down a pot of tea on the table and poured us each a cup. I took note of the color, as it looked more like dirty water then any tea I'd ever known. Mattie and I politely sipped our tea and I felt humbled.

"Well, like I said, I'm a friend of Orange's, and I am sad to be telling you this, but Orange passed away a few months back."

"I sure is sorry to hear that. He was a good man who always traded fairly with me. The last time I saw him, he told me he wouldn't be coming back 'round this side of the mountain, and he left me with extra supplies. You see, I ain't got a truck, and gettin' down the mountain is awful hard with the little ones and all."

Mattie had mulled over how she would approach this woman with charity without wounding her pride. It was after a short pause while everyone was having their own thoughts that Mattie said, "Ma'am, I mean

Miss Shelby, Orange was a God-fearing man who left behind a last will and testament. It had instructions as to what he wanted done with his goods and wares from his traveling days. He mentioned you specifically, Miss Shelby, and we are here to fulfill his wishes. I hope you can accept the goods we have on behalf of Orange, and we would also like you to know that Orange wished for any unpaid debts from your account to be wiped clean."

Well, as you can well imagine, the woman just sat there patting her young baby nervously in her lap, not knowing exactly what to think. Maybe she thought her prayers had been answered; maybe she was just relieved to know we weren't trying to collect money she didn't have. But either way, she looked relieved. This was probably the only time anyone would ever give her something for nothing, and it took a few minutes for it to sink in. But once it did, she seemed less frail and sickly than when we first came calling.

She told Mattie that she was very grateful for our kindness, as her husband had gone off to find work and she hadn't seen him since. She started to cry, as she said she didn't know if he was dead or alive or just run off on her and the kids. We sat there at the table and let her cry it all out, as we knew she had a lot of worries on her shoulders.

After Miss Shelby let out all her bottled-up tears, we told her we had some supplies in the truck for her and the children, and Mattie asked if we could come callin' again in a few months' time to see how she was fairing. Miss Shelby said she would be happy for the company and cried again, but this time it was tears of joy.

So, with a new lightness in her step, Miss Shelby and her kids headed for the truck. Even John Jack could feel the excitement as we all worked unloading the goods. The kids smiled from ear to ear as they thanked us for the food and toys.

Needless to say, we left that afternoon feeling on top of the world.

Heading back to the other side of the mountain, I fell asleep dreaming about those kids and their big smiles. It was dark when we got home, and Mattie went into the house with John Jack to start supper while I unloaded the empty crates in the barn. No sooner did I lift the first crate from the truck bed when I heard an owl hooting from the big 'ole oak tree. Shivers ran up and down my spine as I stood frozen in my tracks, and although it was bitter cold outside, I felt warm inside as my heart swelled thinking of Orange.

A few days later, Bobby Joe came calling, and as we all sat on the porch making small talk, I had to wonder if he knew that Orange left us all his goods. Either way, I knew Mattie would not mention it, and thankfully, he didn't ask. He did, however, ask real casual-like, how our trip went to the other side of the mountain.

Mattie looked him straight in the eyes and said just as casual as he had asked, "Just fine, Bobby Joe. Just fine."

"Y'all need to be careful is all I'm saying," said Bobby Joe.

He knew just as well as I did that there was no point in asking Mattie anything else. When she made up her mind to do something, there was no stopping her.

Nothing more was said about the trip, and I reckon he already knew everything anyhow. It sure is hard to keep things quiet in a small town.

Sadly, what we didn't know then was Bobby Joe was right, and our act of kindness would bring us troubles down the road.

THE AWAKENING

Come the following spring, we continued to work around the land, but we all felt a little lonely. Although we had each other, we all really missed Orange. With spring comes a rebirth, yet we did not share that feeling. The sun was shining and there was a fresh scent in the air, yet we could not muster the same enthusiasm for greeting the days.

Eventually we made a trip into town for our own goods, and while Mattie went inside the general store with John Jack, I unloaded the truck. We planned on getting some scraps to make some new clothes for John Jack. While old lady Jenkins was finishing up with a customer, Mattie wandered to the back of the store where the material was stored. Whenever Mattie bought material, we always had to wash it first. The odor of tobacco and pipe from the locals playing checkers and smoking all day clung to the fabric.

And today was no exception. The locals were there minding everyone's business, although old lady Jenkins's husband was keeping them busier than normal. Something was wrong with his senses, and he would roam to and fro mumbling to himself. He picked at imaginary threads on his shirt and kept trying to take a red checker off the game board. The men were getting agitated and told him to go sit himself down out front and leave them alone.

So, as Mattie made her way through a thick layer of smoke, Mr. Jenkins watched me with a vacant look on his face, and I had to wonder where his mind had gone. No sooner than I finished that thought, we locked eyes, and for one brief moment his cloudy expression cleared and we just stared at each other. He seemed to sense my pain, and I realized then he was not the one lost. I was.

Roaming the mountain later that afternoon, I gave thought to my encounter with Mr. Jenkins. *How was it that someone with his kind of troubles was more connected to this world than me?* I seemed to be having a hard time moving on from my grief, but Mattie said the heart heals itself when it's good and ready. I guess I wasn't ready…

Sadly, that summer was just a blur. The days were long, and I could not for the life of me shake the empty feeling I had inside. I was plum tired, and for the first time in my life, I was ready for winter. I longed for the shorter days and quiet nights to think.

I still had not figured out the note Orange left me, but I remembered how Orange always said not to rush the big things. I reckoned when my mind was thinking clearly and not fuzzy with grief, I would figure out the puzzle, and until then, I just needed to figure out how to get through the days.

Thankfully winter started to set in, and Bobby Joe came calling to see if we needed any help 'round the place now that Orange was gone. Although Mattie would normally brush off any help offered, we did need someone to help drag over some large downed trees for firewood. All the years that Mattie spent bent over in the garden was taking their toll on her back. Many a day when she woke, her back was stiff and it would take the better part of the day to loosen up. Thankfully, John Jack enjoyed working in the garden, and Mattie was teaching him everything she knew about the soil and the seeds. He seemed to be a natural like Mattie when it came to understanding the earth.

Bobby Joe helped pull the trees over, and Mattie made him a nice meal to take home with him that day. Sure enough, the next week, he showed up again to help us 'round the place. After a while, Mattie started inviting him to eat supper with us, and I as I always suspected, they got along right good.

One evening after supper, Bobby Joe told Mattie that the family we helped out on the other side of the mountain moved away last week.

"Shelby left? Where you reckon she went?"

"Rumor has it her husband died working in the coal mines and she had to go live with her sister's family. She couldn't make it by herself, not with the little ones and all."

"I sure is sorry to hear that. She was a good woman, tired and run down, but a good mother," said Mattie.

"Mattie, you make getting by look easy. Y'all are truly blessed. You always have food on the table and a roof overhead."

"I ain't had one easy day since the day I was born," Mattie said, irritated.

Funny thing, though, when Mattie turned her head away from Bobby Joe, I could have swore I saw a slight smile on her face.

＊

One gloomy evening after laboring all day, I walked down the worn path to my special place and sat under a large weeping willow to collect my thoughts before heading in for the night. A light drizzle came down and I looked up at the weeping willow with its drooping branches, and I felt safe sitting under its canopy of leaves. It was a strong tree, deeply rooted in the soil, yet it had a sad feel to it. Maybe the branches sagged from the burden of all it had seen through the many years it lived. It made me wonder if I would ever walk tall again or if the sadness I felt inside would weigh me down for the rest of my days. Whatever it was, I felt comforted by the fact that I was not the only one.

A light rain started to come down and I pulled my knees to my chest, not ready to leave my thoughts quite yet. Raindrops made their way through the leaves, dropping onto my back in a pitter-patter rhyme, almost like the willow was weeping with me. Just as I was about to leave, I heard rustling leaves from trail down below. Instinctively, I sat still and waited to see what it was. It was then I heard the voices.

"You ain't right in the head."

"Then whose idea was it to come up here? Mine, my idea!"

"Shut your mouth—"

"Jesse, that woman comes into town and buys lots of supplies. It don't seem hard times have found her or that mangy gang she calls family."

"I hope you is right, Buddy … "

I sat still as a possum playing dead. Only my eyes moved as I watched the strangers talking. Their overalls were caked in mud, and dark circles under bloodshot eyes marked the sign of drinkers. Although neither was carrying a shotgun, one of the men had a switchblade that he absent mindedly flicked open and closed while talking.

The rain come down harder now, and the sound of the raindrops hitting my back as I sat hunched under the willow seemed so loud, but in reality it was only because I was scared of being discovered. Thankfully, they never noticed.

Sitting on the downed log for a minute, they spoke quietly, planning their attack on our land. I strained to hear what they were saying, but it was no use. The rain came down in sheets, muffling all their words before the winds could carry them my way.

My own thoughts then wandered to Mattie and John Jack. I knew Mattie would be preparing for supper at that time, and John Jack would probably be out in the barn. The sun was starting to set and Mattie had to be wondering at this point why I wasn't back.

I sure didn't like the fact that they was sitting in my special place … my place, where I think on my life and dream big dreams. These men scared me. Desperate times make people do desperate things. My knees slightly trembled and I held them tighter to my body. *Think, Child!*

I would need to beat them boys up the mountain without using the trail and warn Mattie. The thought of them catching my kin unaware made my skin crawl.

Just as the sun faded behind the mountain ridge and darkness crept into my little hollow, the strangers sat up.

"It's time. Let's head up the trail and keep your mouth shut!"

As the strangers made their way up the trail, I sat motionless until I felt it was safe to move. I would have to make my way up through the brush and blackberries if I was to beat them to the top of the mountain. My heart pounded in my chest as I moved snake-like out from under the willow and turned the other direction.

I silently prayed to God to keep Mattie and John Jack safe, all the while trying to send a message of warning to Mattie.

I moved quickly as I parted the brush in front of me, weaving my way through the dense forest. My hands bled from the thorns attacking my bare skin, yet I barely took notice. I had to think hard on what to do, but I worried for Mattie. She could not fend off two men by herself. And so help me God, if those men touched one hair on John Jack's head, I would kill them, kill them right dead. I knew this for sure!

I also knew Orange's gun was still in the shed hidden above the door. If those men beat me to the top, I would have to make my way to the shed and get that gun unnoticed.

With every thought I had, I moved that much quicker. Fear was setting in and my boots slipped in the wet soil. I had to dig my fingers into the mud for a firmer grip up the slope. The knees of my overalls were caked in mud as I used my whole body to force myself through the unforgiving landscape.

Reaching the crest of the mountain, I hunkered down for a minute to listen for any noises. I could not afford to get caught first by the strangers, as I knew I might be the only hope for Mattie and John Jack. Hearing nothing but the pounding rain, I said a prayer as I ran out into the open, heading toward the house. Rain pelted my face as I felt the thundering beat of my heart beckoning me forward. Lightning now crackled overhead and just as a loud burst of thunder rumbled through the mountains, I felt a sharp thud on the back of my head and all went dark as I fell to the ground.

I woke with a terrible headache, and for a moment, I thought this had all been a bad dream until I heard their voices.

"Why did you go ahead and do that?"

"I had no choice—"

"Hurting someone was not in the plan—"

"Busting my way in here and only finding stew on the stove was not what I had in mind neither."

Sharp pains in my head sliced through the foggy feeling I felt as I lifted my head slowly from the wood floor. Peering into a pool of blood, I cupped my hands around my head to keep from fainting. The strangers noticed I had come to and quickly dragged me into the front room by my overalls. Waves of unease filled my body as I fought to hold my insides from spilling out. I tried to get hold of my thoughts, but the pounding in my own head slowed down my reasoning, and speaking out loud seemed a task too large to overcome.

"Y'all got any money 'round here?"

Banging in the kitchen set off a new wave of pain in my head and all I could muster was a groan.

"Buddy, look through all the coffee cans. They gotta have something…"

The thought of John Jack and Mattie somewhere in the house and needing me gave me strength to lift my head and take a look around. As the boys were in the kitchen rummaging through the wares, I remembered what one of them said. *All they found was stew cooking on the stove!* That meant Mattie sensed something was wrong when I was not home come dark and headed out to find me. I gave God thanks and wondered what I should do. I did not want them to work their way upstairs to my room and find the money Mama had been sending us for years.

I summoned all the strength I had and said, "All the money we have is hid out in the shed," I mumbled.

They immediately stopped all the banging and walked over to me, looking down on me like I was a helpless, wounded animal. The one boy had a smirk on his face that I'll never forget. It gave me the willies, and if I had the strength, I would have kicked in all his teeth right then and there. Orange taught me long ago that a wounded animal is unpredictable and dangerous, and I planned on being just that.

"Well, git on up then!"

He pulled at my overalls and I fought a wave of dizziness as I got to my feet. They seemed pleased with themselves as they followed me to the front screen door. I slowly opened the door and peered off into the darkness, trying to collect my thoughts. My body was weak as I slowly put one foot in front of the other and made my way across the front porch. One of the boys had the lantern and it cast an eerie shadow in front of me as I shuffled my feet down the steps hoping not to fall.

"Come on now, hurry yerself up," shouted one of the boys as he poked me in the back with his knife.

Ignoring them, I scanned the mountain for any sign of Mattie and John Jack. The barn doors were closed up and there was no sign of the dogs. They must have gone looking for me, either on foot or in the truck.

I didn't rightly know what I would do if I couldn't get my hands on that shotgun, but I was getting a bit irritated with these boys coming on our land and bossing me 'round like they owned the place. My head still throbbed, but now I was downright mad, and with every step I took, I got a bit stronger as my fear faded. *Hadn't we been through enough this year?* The wind picked up, swirling around me as if the mountain understood that I was in danger, and with the wind, came courage.

Ever since Orange died, I had been struggling to cope with everyday life, and right then it was as if someone was lifting me up and giving me strength I didn't know I had. My head stopped throbbing, my pulse slowed, and I actually felt light in my step.

I barely noticed the owl hooting in the distance, and with a smile on my face, I said, "You boys is dumber than a bunch of rocks, ain't you?"

That stopped them dead in their tracks, as the one boy said, "What'd you just say to me?"

Turning back to look them square in the eyes, I said, "You boys are wasting your time up here looking for money that you know we don't have, cracking open my head like a watermelon, and acting the fool!"

Turning around, I reached for the shed lever to open the door, and in one quick movement I grabbed the shotgun from overhead, pointing it straight at them hillbillies. My voice was strong and sure as I said, "How dare you come up here and try to take what's rightfully mine! I killed a boy up here for trespassing years ago, and I won't hesitate to do it again!"

The boys had that shocked look on their faces as the one who held the switchblade now watched me as I pulled back the hammer on the gun.

"You get off my property or I will drop you right here and now!"

Blood soaked my hair and ran down my face, blurring my vision, but I held onto the cold steel of the shotgun, knowing it was all I had.

It was then I heard a noise from behind the strangers and I looked over the boys to see fuzzy images of Mattie, John Jack, and Sheriff Bobby Joe all pointing their guns at the boys who dared trespass on our land. I couldn't help but smile as the mountain cavalry had arrived and not a minute too soon.

As Bobby Joe yelled at the boys to get on the ground, I locked eyes with Mattie. Knowing that I was now safe, I could feel my hold on the shotgun relaxing as it slipped slowly from my fingers to the ground. At the same time that Bobby Joe was hand-cuffing the strangers, my own weakness took over and it was the last thing I remembered as my world slowed down and I floated far, far away.

I woke the next day to find myself in my bed with a pounding headache. I struggled to lift my head off the pillow, but it was no use; my body was too weak. My efforts woke John Jack, who had been sleeping in the chair next to my bed and who now quickly called out for Mattie.

"Don't move too quick," he said. "Looks like you took quite the lickin' last night."

I cupped my hands around my head and felt the bandages wrapped tightly, holding my thoughts together. I tried to speak, but my voice was raspy and my throat felt dry as a desert. Mattie walked in the room and immediately sat next to me on the bed.

"Child, you gave us quite the scare last night. How does you feel?"

Pulling her face close to mine, I whispered in her ear, "How did you know, Mattie? How did you know something was wrong?"

"I sensed it, Child. I just sensed something wasn't right. I got this strange feeling in the pit of my stomach while I was cooking supper. Then, when it got dark and you weren't home, I knew something was wrong. I got the dogs and John Jack and we headed down the mountain to fetch Bobby Joe."

I told Mattie how I was in my special place when they come along the trail. "I tried to beat them up the mountain to warn y'all, but they knocked me out on the way to the house. The whole way up the mountain, I thought about you and John Jack, praying you would sense something and you did. Thank God you did, Mattie," I said.

"Kin folk always know when something ain't right, Child. You was brave last night and I couldn't be prouder."

My throat was parched as I struggled to say, "They wanted our money, Mattie—"

"I know, Child, I know. John Jack, run and fetch the doc for me, Bobby Joe too."

Mattie fussed on me and gently lifted my head for me so I could sip some water. It felt like liquid heaven, and I gulped it down, immediately feeling better.

"You rest your eyes for a few minutes. The doc wanted to see you again when you woke."

"You called in the doc last night?" I said surprised.

"Yes, Child, Your head was split open and he had to give you stitches last night."

"I have stitches on my head?"

"Sorry to say you do. You also got a bump on the back of your head the size of a small grapefruit. Rest now, Child, and I'll be here when you wake."

I gratefully closed my eyes and fell asleep right off. It seemed like only seconds before everyone was standing in my room again, hovering over me, and urging me to wake up.

"Child, it's Doc Austin here. Do you remember me fixing you up last night?"

"No, sir, I reckon I don't."

"Well, you took a nasty beating to your head and I had to put a few stitches in your scalp. You also got some swelling due to the injury, but I figure with some rest, you'll be fine. Is your head hurting right now?"

"It's pounding something fierce and I got a bad headache," I said.

"Well, let's take another look at it, if you don't mind. I'd also like to change the bandages again, but first I want you to take this pill. It'll help with the pain and the throbbing."

I swallowed the pill on the first try, even though I had never taken a pill before and my throat was sandy feeling. Doc Austin carefully unwrapped the dressing around my head and inspected the stitches, obviously pleased with his work. His hands were large and comforting as he confidently tended to my wound. He asked me a lot of questions that seemed silly, like what day it was, and stuff like that, but I reckoned he was just trying to be friendly. He spoke just above a whisper, and before long his voice seemed to be lulling me back to sleep. I struggled to keep my eyes open, but it was no use. I was drifting off again ...

My dream was fuzzy and unclear. *The moon was bright and the mountain air was foggy but still ... Too still. Nothing moved. No nighttime critters seemed to be out except me and the lone wolf. He looked at me with his glowing eyes from across the pond and just watched. His breathing was fast but steady as I saw his chest rise and fall under the moon's glow. Steam rose from his warm body against the cold air and he waited. I dared not move a muscle as I stood frozen, mesmerized by his presence. He pawed at the ground, eager to come forward, yet he never made a move to advance toward me. Against all my better judgment, I locked eyes with him, staring deep into his soul, and then I understood why he'd been coming 'round all these years. I yelled out to him that he couldn't scare me no more. "Go home," I said. "I know you feed off my own fears."*

He knew I knew; it was all over.

Slowly he hunkered down as he retraced his steps back into the woods, never turning his back to me.

He lived in those woods, coming out only at night, and now I knew why. My fear of death brought him to me all these years. Now that I had a better sense of myself, something told me I would not see him again for a while.

I woke with a deep sense of relief. The haze I had felt in the dream was all but gone and my mind was clear. Lying in bed, I reached for my special box and carefully opened it, revealing my treasures. I immediately rubbed my emerald stone and reflected on my nighttime adventures, like I had done so many times. Replaying the dream in my head, I knew now that the lone wolf that had invaded my dreams in the past represented the demons I felt within. Now that I had confronted those fears, he would not be returning, at least not any time soon. By looking him dead in the eyes, I accepted my own destiny, which then rendered him powerless.

I rested for days before I felt like I had the strength to get out of bed. My headache felt better and the lump was smaller too. Doc Austin checked on me every day and said I was healing right fine. He said he was very surprised to hear I held a gun to them boys or even walked to the shed after taking such a hit to my head.

"I'll tell you what, Child, I have tended to grown men who have taken a hit like you and they were out for good. To think you stood up to them boys with an injury like that is a small miracle. You got some angels watching over you, that's for sure!"

Those words meant more to me at that time in my life than the doc would ever know. I had been feeling beat down all summer, trying to come to terms with Orange's passing. I struggled with my new life, trying not to lose my footing in this world, and then this happened. It's like those boys knocked me out of my fog and I was seeing clearly again.

I now knew that I had not been alone that night. The strength I had mustered to confront them came from above. I reckoned sometimes you had to be knocked down so you could see what's really important. I did have the fire in me, and I just needed to be reminded that I was stronger than I was acting. I let my grief take over and it was high time to get back to living. Orange would have wanted that and he would have understood too.

I took things easy for the next week, and although my body was aching from my injuries, my heart felt much fuller than it had in a long while. I once again took pleasure in the small things like reading by the fire at night. I felt like I was on my way of truly healing from Orange's passing. I got a letter from Mama telling me how sorry she was to hear about my run-in with the strangers. Mattie and John Jack sent her a note, days after my ordeal, explaining what had happened and that I was going to be fine. She said as soon as winter was over, she was planning on coming back to the mountain for a visit. It had been a good many years since we had seen her in person and we all were excited about her upcoming trip. With winter just setting in, we had plenty of time to prepare for our family reunion. Mama sent money as usual and pleaded with me to buy something special for myself as a get well gift from her. I reckoned I would have to think on that one for a while, because for the life of me, I couldn't think of anything I needed. I felt content for the first time in a good while, and I was happy to have that feeling more than anything else in the world.

Strangely, just like tragedy brought Orange into our lives so many years ago, we now felt a special kinship with Bobby Joe. Without his help, those strangers might have hurt me worse or taken everything we had to our name. I overheard Mattie tell him she could never repay him for helping me that night. She said her heart would have surely broken in two if she had lost me. I watched as she wiped tears from her eyes and held Bobby Joe's hands real tight. For a moment, they stood there staring deep into each other's eyes, communicating without words. Their friendship had deepened and I knew they would be the best of friends from that day on.

Bobby Joe said those men had spent a few days in his jail before being sent out of town for a while. Come to find out they had come from the other side of the mountain, and that's why I did not recognize them. They lived close to Shelby and had heard about us helping her and her kids. Anyhow, what they did was wrong, but they also woke me up to life again, and for that I was grateful. I told Bobby Joe as much and he said he understood.

Winter came and went like no time had passed. We were truly a family again and it felt good. We worked side by side on the land and in the house. Christmas was quiet and wonderful as we reflected on our years with Orange. Now when we talked about him it felt comforting instead of painful. It was now just the three of us and we settled into our new life with ease.

Mama mailed us a beautiful new painting of Orange she had been working on since his passing. It was absolutely beautiful and captured his essence perfectly. It was a painting of him standing by the clothesline on the first day Mama met him. The clothes on the line flapped in the breeze just like I remembered on that day. Orange had one hand hooked in his overalls and one arm around my shoulder. You could see in his face the protective feeling he had for me, like a father would have for his child. Dust swirled around us, giving the painting a gritty feel, so true to the feeling of that morning. I was brought back to that morning and I lost myself in the painting for a few minutes. How amazing that Mama remembered such small details of everyday moments. I hung the painting in my bedroom so I could see it every morning when I woke. I had been blessed in my life and I could count on one hand the things I treasured the most, and that painting was surely one of them.

NEW BEGINNINGS

S pring was absolutely beautiful and beckoned us to work outside while we enjoyed the clean fresh mountain air. We toiled in the garden and worked the land with renewed energy and purpose. Mama was coming to visit and everything had to be perfect. I planted flower seeds along both sides of the road coming up the mountain in celebration of Mama's visit. The seeds were an assortment of colors and flowers, wild in their beauty, and a lovely way to honor a visitor of such importance. As the days grew closer to Mama's visit, the flowers opened up and you couldn't help but be drawn into their natural splendor.

John Jack was nervous and excited to see Mama, and the night before she was to arrive on the train, he asked me if I thought Mama would like him. I looked at him and wondered how he could worry about such a thing. But he was, after all, just eight years old, a mere child who had not felt his mama's arms around him for a very long time, and I understood his concerns.

"John Jack, you are the sweetest, most beautiful child I have ever seen, and Mama is going to love you!"

The smile stayed on his face as he curled up next to me and fell asleep.

We picked Mama up at the train depot and she ran into our arms as soon as she saw us. She cried buckets of tears as she held us tight, running her hands through our hair. She smelled like flowers and my mind drifted back many years, just like I remembered. Mama had a glow about her as she held us again. Mattie graciously stood back for a few minutes, letting Mama love on us until she joined our circle.

Mama then turned to Mattie and said "It is good to see you, dear friend!" and they hugged while we stood back this time. We all held hands as we walked to the truck, a family once again. She kept looking at John Jack and commented on how much he had grown and how handsome he was. John Jack was beaming, and it felt good to have us all together again. We felt strong; I felt it in the air.

Driving up the mountain was a pleasure as I watched Mama take in all the flowers.

"How absolutely gorgeous!"

"I planted them for you, Mama," I said.

"Child, thank you very much. This is the nicest welcome I think I have ever had."

We feasted that evening with everyone talking at the same time, and we loved every minute of it. John Jack's worries were put to rest right away as Mama was captivated by his looks and personality, just as everyone else was. Mama laughed a lot, which was music to my ears, and she truly looked at ease with herself. Finally, we all moved to the front room where we sat by the fire, and I brought out Orange's box of treasures to show Mama. She was just as surprised as we were the first time we opened the tin.

"So Orange had a baby all his own. I bet he waited his whole life hoping to set eyes on that little girl. What a pretty name, Abby Mae."

"We think so, but I reckon we'll never know for sure," I said. "He took it to his grave."

"Most folks have some kind of secret they take to their grave, Child. Don't mean it's bad, or good for that matter, It just means sometimes life is complicated. Thank the Lord he had all of you. He sure did love you all. That I do know."

I thought on this for a few minutes. I had my own secrets too. I never did tell Mattie how bad I felt after Orange passed. How my body ached or how I cried myself to sleep every night. She never knew that all summer long, I couldn't catch my breath. How I felt this terrible heaviness weighing down on my chest, almost like I had to remind myself to breathe. Nobody but me and Orange knew about the beautiful stone I found in my special place neither. I guess Mama's right. Secrets are just that. Secret for one reason or another.

"Did you find the treasure, Child?"

"I haven't had any time to figuring out the puzzle. It's been busy 'round here since Orange passed."

"Can I help you this week while I am here? Maybe we can figure it out together?"

"That would be great! Orange would have liked that."

We all talked into the wee hours of the night, until we finally made our way to our beds. Mama was sleeping in John Jack's room, and John Jack was sleeping with me in my room. I slept like a baby and woke the next morning to the fresh smell of coffee coming from the kitchen.

I joined everyone in the kitchen for breakfast and then John Jack and I started the morning chores while Mattie and Mama enjoyed the beautiful sunrise sitting on the front porch. I watched them rockin' in the chairs, sipping on hot coffee, and I felt so at peace. We had been through some rough patches as a family, but our love stayed strong, and we came out of it stronger. Mama caught me looking her way and she waved at me, smiling, and I waved back. No words needed … finally.

John Jack proudly showed off our garden and how Mattie taught him to work the soil. Mama was impressed with his natural talent he had for working the land at such a young age. She told him so, and he hooked his thumbs in his overalls, smiling behind his long locks of hair, and it melted Mama's heart.

Later in the day, the two of us sat on the porch and quietly watched John Jack working around the barn.

"He is a wonderful boy. You and Mattie have done right by him. I knew you would. You know, my heart broke that morning I left both of you so many years ago."

"I know it did, Mama. Thank you for John Jack. He is our entire world. Not a day goes by I don't thank you and the good Lord above for bringing him into our lives—"

"It was all meant to work out the way it did. I just didn't know it at the time is all. Sometimes, it's best not to know every detail, and I reckon God wants you to figure things out for yourself," she said.

"Mama, can I show you something in my room?"

"Of course!" Mama said, surprised.

We ran up the stairs like little kids and Mama sat on my bed, admiring Orange's quilt.

I crawled under the bed and pulled out tin after tin filled with money.

"Mama, this here is all the money you have sent us over the years. I got more money than I know what to do with. You should take this home with you—"

"Child, that money is for you and John Jack. Have you never spent a penny of it?"

"I have. I give Mattie a little every year to help out with paying the taxes, and I buy new shoes for everyone when we need them, but other than that, the land provides for us and we don't have much need for it."

Mama started laughing as she pulled me close. "Child, you are something else! That money is yours and John Jack's. It will come in handy one day and you'll be glad you have it."

"I reckon I'll have to take your word on that, Mama. I am curious about one thing though."

"What's that, Child?"

"I been wondering if you found someone special to share your life with?"

"Sometimes I think I have, but the feeling always fades over time. I think it's best I just live my life for me. I have my painting. I look forward to that every day, and that feeling never does goes away."

"I like that … you found your callin'."

"I like it too, Child. It took a good while, but it was worth the wait."

Sadly, Mama's visit was almost over and it seemed like she just got there. The week had flown by and we all started dreading her leaving the mountain. Mattie and Mama spent every morning on the porch while we did chores. They truly enjoyed each other's company and never seemed to run out of conversation. Bobby Joe came by one morning and joined them for coffee. Mama could sense their deep friendship, and after he left, Mama said, "He is a good man, Mattie."

"That he is," Mattie said as she rocked back and worth in her chair. "He has always been very kind to us."

"Has he asked for your hand in marriage?"

"Oh, good Lord, no! I am too old for that kind of nonsense. No, my life is here with the children, and that's all I need," said Mattie.

Mama just rocked in her chair with a smile on her face. *Seems like everyone has found their place, now we just get to sit back and enjoy watching John Jack find his,* thought Mama.

Later that day, Mama and me took a walk to my special place to talk. A slight breeze wound its way through the canopy of trees and my tin strips danced in front of us. Mama then leapt up from the log and said, "That's it! Orange said to listen to the music! Was Orange's harmonica in the tin box with the note?"

"No, it wasn't," I said. "That's funny...I never noticed it was missing."

"You will find the treasure when you find that harmonica!"

"Mama, do you think he hid it in the shed?"

"I think we are about to find out. Let's go!"

We held hands as we ran up the trail and headed for the shed. I carefully opened the shed door and immediately glanced above to see Orange's shotgun right where it belonged. It brought me comfort, just as it did to see it that fateful night. Mama and me sat on the bed and scanned the small shed for clues. I looked under the bed, on the work bench, and behind the stove. Nothing! The dirt floor was bumpy but smooth, just as I remembered it years ago. Nothing seemed out of place.

"I don't get it, Mama. I don't see anything."

"Maybe we should have some sweet tea and think on it some more."

We settled on the front porch, sipping tea and thinking on the riddle. I got out the tin and read out loud the riddle again hoping for inspiration.

"Be still your thoughts, Child,
and listen to the music.
Hidden for years past
Where thoughts are lulled
Is a treasure unlike any other."

As I rocked back and forth, it came to me.

"Mama, it's right here! This is where Orange played music at night and where the rocking chairs lull you into your thoughts."

"You're right, Child! It's been right here all along!"

We both jumped up from our chairs and ran down the porch steps. Calling Pudro out from under the porch, I then crawled into his space. It smelled like dog, musty and dank. The first thing I found was one of John Jack's marbles he had been looking for and I put it in my back pocket. Lying on my belly,

I called out to Mama and said, "What exactly am I looking for?"

"Is there anything out of place or a marker of some kind?"

"Not that I can see. I am going to crawl farther back and see if anything stands out."

So there I was, shuffling about on all fours and laughing to myself, thinking that Orange must be enjoying this. He always loved a good puzzle, just like me. My hands were dusty from skimming the dirt floor, and yet I found nothing. I wondered if I had this all wrong. Nothing was here, and as I turned to leave, I sat up a little too much and my head hit the underside of the porch. I automatically rubbed my head and looked up to see that I had hit a support beam for the porch, and what do you know! My eyes widened as I peered upon a large tin strapped to the beam, just waiting for me to find it!

"Mama, I found it! I found it! Can you get Mattie?"

Mama ran into the barn where John Jack and Mattie were working and told them of the find. Everyone ran back to the porch and I asked Mattie for her pocketknife. John Jack eagerly crawled under the porch and cut the strap that held the treasure safely for so long while Pudro barked over and over again, somehow knowing the importance of the find.

That evening, we all sat by the fire after supper and Mattie handed me the key that fit the lock box. This time, my hands did not shake. Orange left this for me, and I couldn't wait to open the box and see what he wanted me to have.

The harmonica was wrapped in a note from Orange that said:

Child,

Your dreams were always my dreams too. I reckon that's how it is when you is a papa. Dream big, Child ... dream big.

Orange

I sat holding the letter and thought it was the most precious thing ever.

No more words needed.

I then looked into the large tin and found sealed envelopes. I opened the first one to find money, and lots of it! Bill after bill neatly stacked and wound in string. The next envelope held the same, and so on and so on ... a lifetime of working was in these envelopes. What a splendid life indeed!

Mattie spoke first and said, "Child, I can't believe Orange had all this money. I had no idea."

"He didn't care one bit about the money. He only cared about us," I said.

"You is right about that, Child," said Mattie.

I did not realize then how much money that was or how it made me rich. In fact, many years would pass before I come to see how much money I had. Mattie and Mama understood the value of the treasure, but to me it was just more money I would hide under my bed for a rainy day. My real treasure was the note from Orange.

Anyway, between the money Orange left me and the money Mama sent every week for last nine years, I had accumulated quite a small fortune.

Sadly, we had to say goodbye to Mama that summer. We didn't want her to leave, and John Jack in particular did not want her to go, but we knew she would never stay.

A few days after Mama left town, Bobby Joe came calling, just as he had every week since Orange passed. Physically, he and Mattie could not do any heavy lifting no more, and so that was left to John Jack and me. Mattie's back still ached her something bad, and I knew it was even worse than she let on. Many a night I would put a warm cloth on her back to ease her sore muscles. One night, as we sat by the fire, Mattie fell asleep and I took a good look at her. Her hair, which was once thick and light brown, was now light grey and wiry looking. Her face was tired, with wrinkles lining her forehead, and often her ankles were swollen from the day's chores. I knew she was aging and it broke my heart. When Orange passed I was still just a child and I didn't know how quickly the years could add up, but now I was older and understood.

And then, in a blink of an eye, or so it seemed, Mattie stopped working outside all together. Even hanging the laundry on the clothesline was too taxing for her back. John Jack and I continued to do all the chores with Mattie tending to the house and the cooking. Often during the day, I would catch Mattie napping by the fire and I would take pause and watch her. Although Mattie appeared old, she actually seemed more like a child to me than ever before. Lately, I could see my role changing, as now it was time to take care of her, like she did for me so many years ago.

Years passed with the three of us still on the mountain and living off the land. John Jack was twelve years old and looked more like a young man than a child. He still had his whole life ahead of him, but for others, the years brought change of a different kind.

Bobby Joe retired and his replacement was a deputy from a neighboring town. His name was T. Wilson and he had a wife and two kids. He seemed nice enough, but it was not the same. Bobby Joe was one of a kind, and filling his shoes would be no easy task. He still lived in town in the small house he once shared with his late wife. Whenever I made my trips into town, I always stopped by to visit with him, finding him on his front porch watching over the town he protected for most of his life.

Mrs. Jenkins's husband passed, and within a year, she sold the general store and moved across the county line to live out her final years with her younger, widowed sister. Mrs. Jenkins had been tending to her husband's ills for many years, and although she loved him deeply, you could sense she had been set free as well.

Her living quarters were attached to the store and behind a door marked "Private—Keep Out." All those years, she lived her life inside one building, just moving from the front of the store to the back. She once told me she longed for a garden to tend to and dreamed of a house with a white picket fence. I hope her sister had at least one of those for her. She deserved it after all these years.

The husband and wife who took over the store moved from out of state, and although the locals were none-too-friendly toward outsiders, most folks had no choice, as they did run the only store in these parts. Thankfully, they were God-fearing people who were seen every Sunday at church, and this put the town folk at ease.

One evening as we all sat by the fire, John Jack was talking about his plans for the garden this coming spring, when Mattie said, "You always got to plan ahead, that's for sure." Years ago, I remember Mattie telling me that you got to have dreams to take you into the future. It got me to thinking, lately, now that Mattie was aging and all, that it was important I step forward and guide our family as best as I could.

"Mattie, John Jack, what do you think about buying the Parsons' land? If we did, we would own most of the mountain ridge."

John Jack immediately put his book down and Mattie looked up over her glasses, letting her knitting needles fall in her lap before she said, "Child, what would we do with all that land? We can barely take care of what we have right now—"

"We could rent out the house to help cover the taxes while we still would have all the land on the mountain for ourselves. Or maybe we could find a family in need and trade rent for help around here. That way we get an extra hand but have the benefit of owning the land for years to come."

"Actually, that's not a bad idea, Child. Not bad at all. I like the idea of renting to a nice family who could help you and John Jack 'round our place."

"What do you think, John Jack?"

"I like it. We could always use some help, especially come winters when we have so much wood to haul."

"Well, that's that then! I will make a call on the bank next week and see how much they want."

"Good," said Mattie. "That's that!" Mattie went back to knitting with a smile on her face, knowing I was dreaming us into the future.

The following week I paid a visit to the local bank to ask about the Parsons' land.

I stood before the bank's large wooden doors and took pause. I knew I was dreaming us into the future and I wanted to remember this moment. The butterflies in my stomach fluttered with nervous excitement as I took a large breath and reached for the iron door handle. Pulling open the doors, I felt myself stepping into the future and I knew Orange would approve. We were starting a new chapter in our lives, and all I could do was smile. I also couldn't help but be taken aback by the banker man as he approached me. He was a very large man, balding, and his suit seemed too small for his body. The buttons on the front of his jacket looked ready to pop off at any minute, as the material gathered tightly around his swollen stomach.

I introduced myself and he motioned to a chair for me to have a seat.

"What can I do for you today?"

"I am here to see about buying the Parsons' land," I said.

The banker seemed amused and asked how I was figuring to pay for the land, being I had no bank account with him.

I said, "With cash."

The banker's chair squeaked as his posture changed and he leaned forward now to get a good look at me. He wiped away small sweat beads on his forehead with a white handkerchief as a fan droned on behind him, moving around the already warm air. Looking at me now in a different way, he carefully said, "Well then, let's take a look at the books, shall we?"

I watched as he fumbled through his ledger book until he came to the page he was wanting. His bald head shimmered in the sunlight coming through the glass as he bowed it closer to see the figures. He would look at me and then look at his book with a serious scowl on his face as he pondered the price.

Orange taught me long ago that when you is making a deal, you got to let things unfold naturally.

He'd say, "Child, folks like to talk, but when they is talking, they ain't thinking. You got to take your time is all."

So that's what I did. The banker kept looking to me as if I would show my hand, and I never did. I took my time, and after some bargaining back and forth, we came to an agreement on the price. I promised to return the following day with the money and we shook hands.

That was that.

I returned the next day as promised, bringing the money in a coffee can, which I set down on the banker's desk. He looked surprised and happy all at the same time as I signed my name on the deed to the land.

"You know, I didn't think you would come back."

"When you get the chance to do something big, we owe it to ourselves to at least try."

"You sure is right about that."

I left the bank that day feeling that I had just invested in John Jack's future, and it felt good…real good. We now owned most of the mountain ridge.

That evening, I wrote Mama and told her of the good news. Later, when I crawled into bed, I curled up in Orange's quilt and thanked him for the land. It was, after all, his dream too.

The following morning after breakfast, Mattie and me drove the truck into town while John Jack did chores. We stopped by Bobby Joe's place so Mattie could visit for a while and I could see if Bobby Joe knew of any family who might want to rent our house.

Before I could even bring up the subject, Bobby Joe said, "I hear you bought the Parsons' land—"

"Some things never change, even after you retire!" I said. "Well, since you spoiled my surprise, do you by any chance know of a family that might be a good fit for us to rent out the house?"

"I do know the church is helping out a few families in need. You might want to drop by and talk with them about your situation."

I left the two of them on the porch to catch up while I headed to the church. Once inside, I lit a candle and left a penny for my thoughts. After praying for my family, I found Preacher Matthew and told him of my idea.

"Can you think of anyone that might work out?" I asked.

"I have a few families that are in need of a helping hand, but one in particular might be perfect for you" he said.

"Tell me about them."

"The family's name is Graham, and they are from the other side of the valley. They lost their farm a few months back and have been living off the kindness of neighbors and the church, in which they have been doing odd jobs in exchange for a place to sleep. The dad, Rush, and the mama, Emma, have three kids.

The eldest boy, Junior, is about fourteen years old and has two younger sisters, Pearl and Lily. They are God-fearing folks, hard working, and proud. I think they might be a good fit for you."

"I think so too. Are they around today?"

"They are. Have a seat and I'll go fetch them."

I was lost in thought when I heard the familiar sound of the church floor buckling and squeaking behind me. I turned to find a lovely-looking family, poor and proud, staring back at me.

Preacher Matthew introduced us all and then said he would be out back if we needed him.

"I don't know how much you have been told, but I am looking for a family to live on land owned by my family, rent free, in exchange for some help 'round our own place ... "

I watched the family carefully as they thought on what I said. The girls had no idea what was going on while the older boy stood tall next to his mama. She was a slight woman who was used to hard work, judging by her hands. The dad was stocky and tall, with large hands that he protectively rested on his wife's shoulder.

"We mainly need help during the winter downing and hauling wood, but we also could use some general help every day," I said. "I have a brother who is a bit younger than your boy who could use an extra pair of hands to help out. We live at the top of the mountain and the land you would be living on is halfway up along the ridge.

"We appreciate the offer, but we have no means of buying seed or supplies to get started," said Rush.

"I figured we could buy you supplies until you get settled. This ain't charity by any means. The land needs work, and I have never even been inside the house. It's been empty for years and will need a lot of work to get it in shape."

Rush gave this some thought before saying, "I reckon we could try it for a spell and see if the arrangement works out. The wife and I could work the land while our boy helps you out on your place. How's that sound?"

"Perfect! Now let's gather your belongings before it gets too late in the day and head over to the general store to get you some supplies."

Emma looked overjoyed and nervous as she hustled the girls outside to say goodbye to Preacher Matthew before we all headed out to their new home.

After stocking up with supplies, we picked up Mattie and headed back up the mountain.

"Child, you did good...real good. I liked them the minute I set eyes on them."

"Me too, Mattie."

For the first time in my life, I turned left off the mountain and wound my way down the road to the Parsons' place. The house was in a bad way, and it needed repairs and a family to bring it back to life. It was a decent size, but everything was overgrown around it almost to the point of nature taking back what it once owned. I turned off the truck, grabbed the shotgun from the rack, and headed toward the house with our new neighbors. Emma had a scared look on her face while she took in the sight of her new home, and Rush wiped his forehead with the back of his hand as he surveyed the work ahead.

"Like I said, I ain't never been in this house, so let's take a look around and see what needs to be done," I said.

Strangely, the house was filthy but untouched from the wilds growing around it. It had a large fireplace, a small kitchen, one room off the back, and wood stairs with a loft area over head. Dirt marks on the walls showed the spot where pictures were long ago displayed. Animal droppings littered the floor and the strong odors of critters living inside invaded our senses, beckoning us to open the windows and let fresh air in.

While Emma began the first steps of airing out the house, Rush and I checked out the barn and found some old furniture and supplies scattered about. Most would have to be thrown away, but some of the scrap could be re-used to fix things up. As we walked back to the house, I noticed, to my horror, a noose hanging from a large oak tree. I stopped dead in my tracks, stricken with pure disbelief as to what I was setting my eyes on. Ivy had wound itself in and around the rope, but there was no denying what it was. My heart raced, and before I could even think straight, I was climbing the tree to rid my world of the evil I saw. I quickly pulled out my pocket knife and went to work on cutting the rope, which eventually fell to the ground with a thud. I clung to the tree as I wondered who could be so wicked and vile to do such a thing. *Was it meant for Orange?* My mind started drifting back many years to that fateful day the Parson boys came on our land looking for Orange, but thankfully, Rush called out to me, bringing me back from my memories. Slowly I shimmied down the tree trunk, never taking my eyes off the noose. I wanted to throw it as far as I could, but I knew this would not erase the memory from my mind. Holding back the tears, I told Rush to burn it after we left. I never touched it, as I figured doing so would be like touching the devil himself.

Mattie once told me that evil exists in this world. I just didn't know it was right there on our mountain.

After inviting the family over for supper, I got back in the truck with Mattie. She took one look at me and asked what was wrong.

I lied and said nothing.

I had never outright lied to Mattie before. I didn't like doing it, but there was no sense in her knowing what I saw. Some ghosts from the past was just too scary to bring up again.

Later that evening, after introductions were made to John Jack, we all sat down and had supper in front of the fire. Mattie had made a fine pot of stew with biscuits and we all ate in silence, hungry after such a long day. It was then that I noticed John Jack paying particular attention to Pearl. She had to be a year or two younger than John Jack, and she seemed unaware of his interest in her. I must say, she was a pretty girl, with pale white skin, long blonde hair, and big green eyes.

She wore a flowered dress with two large pockets in front. Her hair was pulled back in a ponytail with a matching ribbon that had not been there earlier. Her legs were skinny, slightly dirty, and she wore old socks that sagged, hanging over her boots. Yet, with all that, she had a graceful look to her, like her mama. As I sat back and gave the family a good look, I knew I had made the right choice. They was an honest, God-fearing family, and something told me this was all going to work out just fine.

The Grahams got to work the very next day cleaning up the house and the land. They were able to tame the growth clinging to the house, and maybe for the first time ever, the house came to life. The roof leaked, but thankfully the scrap wood and tin found in the barn was used to patch the offending holes. The birds' nests were cleaned out of the chimney and the family was able to now sit by a fire after a long day's work.

John Jack was more than happy to help them get a garden started, providing seed and knowledge of the mountain soil. Every day he sent Junior home with extra corn, carrots, or whatever we had to help feed the family until their garden was producing.

The boys also took to fishing together, and it seemed like John Jack had a new best friend. Mattie was very pleased with the new arrangement and often mentioned how proud she was of me.

"Child, you have done right by this family," she would say.

"Thank you, Mattie. So have you."

Thankfully, the arrangement did work out, and the mountain was once again thriving, but this time under John Jack's direction. The seasons passed quickly with both families working the land, and before I knew it, I was wondering where the past five years had gone. My memories drifted back through the years, when John Jack snapped me out of my thoughts and said, "We got to head to town right now. It's Bobby Joe."

"Bobby Joe? What's wrong?" I said.

"Preacher Matthew found him in his house when he didn't answer the door for his supper."

"Oh, dear Lord ... "

I suddenly felt tired in a way I had not felt just minutes before, and as I turned to open the screen, I was startled to see Mattie standing there staring back at me. The look on her face was one I had not seen even when Orange had passed. This look was different.

Mattie prayed the whole way into town as John Jack and I sat numbly silent. We really didn't know what to expect, and although I wanted John Jack to drive faster, part of me wanted to never get there.

John Jack held Mattie's hand as we made our way to Bobby Joe's front porch. We gently opened the screen door to find Preacher Matthew sitting somberly in the front room. He stood and helped Mattie to a chair.

Kneeling down in front of Mattie and holding her hands, Preacher Matthew explained that Bobby Joe had passed and was with the Lord now. "He looks real peaceful, and I reckon he died in his sleep," he said.

Mattie's chin began to quiver as she took in the news. Tears ran down her cheeks and she wiped them away as she tried to compose herself. Standing, she smoothed down the front of her dress and asked if she could see him.

"Yes, of course. He's in his room."

Mattie looked our way as she followed the preacher into the other room. No words were needed.

Preacher Matthew opened the bedroom door and Mattie's breath was taken away as she saw her dear friend lying in his bed.

"If you would be so kind, as to give me a few minutes alone with Bobby Joe?"

"Of course, I'll be in the front room if you need me."

Preacher Matthew closed the door as he left the room, and Mattie stood frozen from grief.

Looking upon Bobby Joe, Mattie ached for the man she quietly loved. Slowly, she walked to his bedside and gently adjusted the pillow under his head. Kneeling next to his bed, she clasped his hands in hers and patted the back of his hands in an effort to ease his pain. Mattie then whispered in his ear how she had always loved him. "Thank you kindly for your friendship over the years. It truly meant the world to me." Mattie's large tears dropped onto Bobby Joe's face, and it seemed like he was crying with her as she spoke the words she only now found the courage to say. Mattie gave her one and only love, a kiss on the lips and then struggled to get back up.

Mattie left the room the same way she had entered: heartbroken.

I knew this because I dreamed it that very evening. I wish I hadn't, though. Some things is just meant to be secret.

Bobby Joe had no family, and Mattie insisted on paying for his funeral service. I found her on her knees, digging in the dirt under the 'ole oak tree.

"Mattie, what in the world is you doing?"

"Digging up my money…"

"Why does everyone hide their money here?" I asked as I started to help in the digging.

"I reckon most folks won't look in a cemetery."

"That's the same thing Orange said!"

So, we both dug where she knew her money was hid. "I have money, Mattie. I could pay for the service."

"Thank you, Child, but no. I have to do this for Bobby Joe. It's the last gift I'll be able to give him."

Sadly, she was right about that.

The service was simple, just like Bobby Joe would have liked, and the town folk came out in droves to pay respect to the man who protected them for so many years. I couldn't help but think that Mattie looked like the grieving widow. Although she kept to herself, moving along the outskirts of the crowd, I knew she was feeling the weight of the world on her shoulders. After the service, we all traded stories about Bobby Joe and what a great man he was. Later that afternoon, after everyone had left, Preacher Matthew read Bobby Joe's will. It stated that all of his money and his house, which he owned outright, be left to the church. It was then that preacher Matthew handed Mattie an envelope with her name on it. He said it was from Bobby Joe.

That evening, as John Jack and I sat by the fire, Mattie retired to bed early, taking with her the sealed envelope. To this day, I have no idea what it said. I never asked and Mattie never said.

Some secrets are meant to be just that. Secret for whatever reason, just like Mama said.

IT WAS WRITTEN
IN THE STARS

The Grahams were getting along quite well, and the family had been able to save some money over the years as they stayed on the mountain. Junior still worked for us in the mornings, and then he worked in town at the mill with his papa. They hoped to be able to buy their own land within the next couple of years. Although they loved living on the mountain, they dreamed of having their own place again, and I didn't blame them. But our arrangement worked out well for both of us.

John Jack and Pearl seemed to take to each other, and found any kind of excuse to be together. They were both coming of the age to where this did not go unnoticed. They made a handsome-looking couple, and many a day you could find them working the garden together, fishing, or just sitting on the front porch in the early evenings, talking as they watched the sun set.

Mattie, although aging faster now, was still healthy and tended to the cooking and house just like she had for so many years. She hated to show any kind of weakness, so other than her back problems, if she had any ills, she did a good job of hiding it. Mattie told me long ago that hard work and clean living was the key to living a long life. Thankfully, she did both.

One evening, as we all sat by the fire, John Jack asked how we felt about Pearl. Mattie immediately looked in my direction with a smile on her face.

"How do you mean John Jack?" Mattie said.

"Well, I think real highly of her, and every day I set eyes on her, my heart skips a beat."

"You don't say."

"So, I was wondering how you felt."

"John Jack, although I appreciate you taking us into account, what's important is how you feel. But, just so you know, I like her very much. She is a sweet girl who is hard working, and she seems to care for you an awful lot."

Needless to say, we all went to bed that night with different thoughts and dreams.

John Jack had a lot on his mind, and the best way to figure out his thoughts was through hard work. After a few weeks of mulling things over, he came to us one night and said he had made a decision. John Jack said Pearl was the most beautiful girl he had ever laid eyes on, and the thought of not spending every day with her for the rest of his life would surely break his heart. He wanted to marry her and raise a family, and if she said yes, he would consider himself the luckiest man alive.

"Marriage lasts a lifetime," said Mattie. "You are going on eighteen years old, so what I'm asking is do you know in the deepest part of your heart that you want to spend the rest of your life with Pearl?"

"I have no doubt," said John Jack.

"Well then, congratulations," said Mattie.

The following week, John Jack asked Rush for permission to marry his daughter. Rush couldn't have been happier and gave him his blessing.

That evening I put my emerald under my pillow and had the most beautiful dream of John Jack proposing to Pearl on a moonlit night by the pond. *Shooting stars dashed across the sky, but they did not even take note. John Jack's eyes were locked with Pearl's, and all he saw was the love of his life. Tears of joy welled up in Pearl's beautiful emerald eyes and gently rolled down her cheeks as they kissed under the starry night.*

We wrote Mama the following week and told her of the good news. We let her know the wedding was planned for the coming spring. John Jack enclosed a picture of Pearl so Mama could see how beautiful his bride-to-be was.

Mama wrote back immediately and said how pleased she was to hear the news. She also said she was coming out on the train in a few weeks to spend time with all of us and help us with the preparations.

Mama arrived by train and had trunk after trunk with her. She finally had some age to her, but she still turned heads wherever she went. Oh, it felt so good to see her again, and we were all smiles as we loaded the trunks into the bed of the trunk. Mattie was waiting for us at home with enough food to feed the entire town. As we drove down the bumpy road, memories from my childhood come spilling back into the present full force. Soft music started playing in my head, and I was lost in the past. I looked over to John Jack and Mama, who were talking, but I never heard a word. I was completely lost in the moment, and for the first time in my life, I felt completely whole. Whole in a way that I never even knew existed. Slowly, the music faded in my head, and I heard John Jack talking about Pearl as we turned off the road and headed up the mountain.

After some talks with Rush, we all decided that John Jack and Pearl would live in the 'ole Parson house, as the Grahams had saved enough money to buy their own place. Thankfully, they wanted to stay on this side of the mountain to be close to everyone.

That winter, everyone was busy with one project or another. Mattie and Mama worked for hours on end every night making a beautiful wedding quilt for John Jack and Pearl's wedding gift. They decided that the colors of the quilt should reflect the spring-time blooms, as well as the colors of the garden that John Jack lovingly babied for so many years. Scraps of material in yellow, brown, green, red, and of course, orange, were carefully stitched together to make the wedding ring bands. After one evening of sewing for hours, Mama was tired and she mistakenly cut out a wedding ring in orange instead of yellow. After showing Mattie what she had accidentally done. Mattie said, "It's meant to be, Viola. Life ain't perfect, and your mistake is a real reflection of love: beautiful and flawed all at the same time."

"You is right about that Mattie!" Mama said, laughing.

They decided to leave it, and we all thought it was the most interesting part of the quilt.

The quilt design was simple but colorful. It had three rings across that interlocked with each other and three rows, totaling nine wedding bands. Eight were mainly yellow with scraps of other colors and the bottom right ring was orange. Small tulips were sewn on the four corners of the quilt to represent the springtime wedding, and under each tulip Mama hid a gold coin in the batting to represent prosperity in the coming years.

Pearl's folks were also busy preparing for the upcoming changes, and it looked as if Rush had found a nice piece of land on the lower part of the mountain. It had a small house that needed some work, but overall it had good bones and would suit them just fine for years to come.

Pearl's mama was busy making the wedding dress, and although we had not seen it yet, we knew it would be simple and beautiful, just like Pearl.

Emma ordered white fabric from the Sears and Roebuck catalog, and pearl beads were lovingly hand-stitched along the neckline and sleeves.

Winter came and went faster than any winter I had ever known. It was as if the coming nuptial was the most important event in our lives, and we willed the cold months to be over so we could all rejoice come spring. Life seemed to be moving at top speed, and before we knew it, the mountain had come alive, everything was in full bloom, and our spirits soared.

Days before the big event, Mattie and Mama were cooking up a storm. Although the only folks coming were our two families, a few folks from the mountain, and Preacher Matthew, you wouldn't know that by all the food being prepared. This was the biggest event ever on the mountain, and Mattie intended to make this day as special as she could for the young couple.

The night before the big day, Mattie and Mama put the final stitches in the wedding quilt, and we all sat back to admire the beautiful creation they sewed.

It really was a stunning quilt, and we knew it would be treasured for years to come. A letter was written to John Jack and Pearl explaining the meaning behind the quilt design and the hidden coins. Scraps of material were added for any repairs needed in the future, and then Mattie and Mama signed their names.

We all retired to bed early that evening and I fell asleep as soon as my head hit the pillow from pure exhaustion.

I dreamed of clothes hanging on the clothesline drying in the night's warm air, flapping gently in the breeze. *As the shirts moved, I saw the lone wolf on the mountain ridge behind the house watching me. He tilted his head toward the moon and howled in a melodramatic way, filling the silent night with his eerie song. The slight breeze carried with it whispers that I could barely hear. They moved with the wind, swirling in and around me, yet I still could not understand the words. Off in the distance, I heard an owl hoot and then the cry was carried away in the wind. I looked back into the woods and the wolf was gone.*

I woke that morning worried about my dream. I sensed something was wrong, but I didn't understand why the wolf was back. I lay in bed for a few minutes trying to sort out the details before I heard Mattie calling me from downstairs. Although I wanted to think on it some more, we had a busy day and I needed to set my worries aside and get started on my chores.

Later that morning, Mama and me took a few minutes to just sit on the porch and talk before we had to get dressed. I watched large fluffy clouds slowly dance across the blue sky. It was as if the heavens approved of the coming union and the day was blessed from the start. Although we talked about having the ceremony at the town church, John Jack decided that the mountain and Pearl were his two great loves, and it seemed fitting to have the wedding here. The weather was perfect, and thankfully I had all but forgotten about my dream last night.

"I can see why you have been so happy living here," said Mama. "It's beautiful. Even as a child I loved watching the sun rise and set on the mountain. I would take scraps of paper and draw sunsets on them, but my papa would rip them up while laughing, telling me how they didn't even look like a sunset. Then one night, as I sat outside watching another day disappear on the horizon, I painted it in my mind instead. I knew, even as a kid, he couldn't steal my memories. So, from then on out, that's where I kept my pictures, all in my head, where they was safe from him."

"Oh, Mama, I am so sad to hear that. Can you ever forgive him for not being the best papa he could have been?"

"I reckon in some strange way I have. Mind you, I will never forget. Sometimes late at night, thoughts creep into my head that I would rather not remember. Anyhow, over the years, I figured out that his problems shouldn't be mine, and his mistakes should not be my guilt to carry around."

"Mama, after all these years, have you ever gave thought to moving back here?" I asked.

"Sometimes I do think I could be happy here."

"I love you, Mama," I said as I reached for her hand and held it tight just like she had done so many years ago to me.

I was relieved to hear Mama had finally outrun her demons and could see herself living on the mountain again.

Mattie once told me forgiving is hard. She'd say, "You got to dig down deep in your heart, and that takes more courage than giving into anger. And if you don't forgive, you'll sour like old milk."

Well, I reckoned Mama finally was able to forgive her papa for all the things he had done, and not done, I supposed. It might have taken a good many years, but she did it, and that's all that mattered.

That afternoon we all stood dressed in our finest clothes and shined boots waiting for the bride to make her appearance. John Jack stood next to Preacher Matthew looking calm and sure as he was about to embark on the next phase of his life.

Sifting through images in my mind like a picture show, I recalled one memory after another and wondered where all the time went. The years just seemed to fly by, and at that moment, I just stood there trying to figure out how to let go. John Jack was a grown man now, and *how could I say goodbye to the boy who stole our hearts so many years ago? How could I admit to myself that Pearl was now the main love of his life and not Mattie, Mama, and me?* I blushed at the thought of my jealousy, knowing it was a true emotion, and one I was not proud of.

The moment of remembering was gone before I knew it, just like the past years, and I was brought back to the present as I watched Pearl walking toward the love of her life. John Jack was engulfed in her beauty and could not take his eyes off her. Pearl looked stunning in her wedding dress, and she seemed to glide over the ground toward her new life. They held hands as Preacher Matthew started the ceremony and we were all were swept away.

Mama dabbed tissue at the corner of her eyes as she watched her son standing before God, looking like a grown man instead of a boy. Mattie hung onto my arm for support and beamed with pride as she also gazed upon the man who she considered her son.

I reckoned they were both right.

Oh, how I wished Orange was standing beside me watching the wedding of his boy too. I know he would have been proud of the man John Jack had become.

The ceremony was short and sweet and the evening celebrating went on long after dusk. The smell of food cooking on the barbecue lingered in the air while everyone danced the night away.

John Jack and Pearl opened their gifts while we all held our breath, hoping they would like them. Pearl was taken aback by the wedding quilt and ran her hands over the design, knowing how much work went into creating something that beautiful. Mama and Mattie told her the story about the orange wedding ring, and she agreed that it seemed fitting to leave it. Then it came time for my gift, which was nicely wrapped in paper and tied with string. John Jack carefully opened the paper to see the deed of the Parsons' place with his name on it.

"You gave us the house?" he said.

"Yes," I said. "The house and the land too- It's all yours. Free and clear, all you have to do is pay the taxes every year."

Pearl started crying and John Jack thanked me with a bear hug, and it was then I whispered in his ear that this gift was also from Orange. He smiled and said, "Thank you, I have felt him with me all day."

That night, as I lay down to sleep, I thought about my dream and strained to hear any whispers being carried by the evening wind. I heard nothing and fell asleep right quick.

ONE MOMENT
IN TIME

L ife on the mountain got back to normal, and John Jack and Pearl had settled in nicely in their new home. A beautiful clock adorned their fireplace mantle, which was a gift from Pearl's family for their wedding. It had been in the family for years and would continue to be cherished for generations to come.

Although we all slept in different homes, we treated the land as if it was one. Work time was split between our land and theirs, and both properties thrived under John Jack's guidance.

Mama seemed content being on the mountain, and surprisingly, she made no mention of heading back home yet. It felt right having us all together, working together, and being the family we always longed to be.

Life was good, at least for a while.

Then everything changed, changed forever, and there was no way to turn back the hands of time.

The morning started off as normal as it had for years. Mattie was cooking breakfast while I was doing morning chores, and Mama was down the mountain at John Jack's. The winds had picked up and it looked like a spring storm was headed our way.

I worked fast to finish up outdoors and headed toward the house for a nice warm breakfast, ignoring the clothes flapping on the line. The minute I walked inside though, I knew something wasn't right. Burnt bacon was sizzling in a pan, and the house was filled with a thin layer of smoke. I quickly removed the skillet from the stove and called out for Mattie, but got no answer.

I headed toward Mattie's room and stood before her bedroom door, which was slightly open, and I froze. I called out her name and waited—nothing.

My heart quickened as I gently pushed open the door and saw her lying on her bed.

"Mattie?"

"Mattie?" I called.

There are times in your life when you have one moment that changes the course of everything. One moment that defines you, one moment that changes who you are or who you are about to become. One moment that takes you somewhere you have never been.

Sometimes that one moment in your life shifts your world so swiftly and violently that you can feel the very earth beneath your feet groan from the impact of the change. That was one of those moments. My whole life changed forever, and it had just been one moment.

I held on to the door frame, frozen in fear. That moment seemed to last for hours as my mind raced back over the years, reliving fragments of moments that added up to a lifetime.

Then the clocked ticked forward once more and it was over.

I ran to Mattie's side and cradled her in my arms just as she had done many years before with her own mother. I stroked her hair, kissed her cheek, and rocked her frail body with all my love. I did not beg for her life as I did many years ago with Orange, because now I knew better. I did not pray to the good Lord above, asking him to bring her back, because now I knew better. I did not wish for another day with my dear Mattie, because now I knew. Sadly, I knew it would not change that moment in time. It was not mine to change. It had been planned from the minute Mattie had been born that this was her moment and hers alone.

Slowly, I curled up to Mattie, just as I had done many years before with Orange, and I held her. Her moment was gone, and now it was my time to say goodbye.

My heart sorted through images of Mattie, and I wondered, *did I remember everything? Every moment I had the chance to give a hug or a smile, did I? Did I tell Mattie today how much I loved her? Did she know, even when I let the moment pass me by, how much I cared for her? Lord knows I hope so ... I hope she knew.* My thoughts slowed and my grief took over, plunging me into the darkness I felt so many years ago with Orange. As my tears flowed, the sky darkened and rain started to come down hard, and it all seemed fitting. The mountain was crying along with me, knowing it had lost one of its own.

All, in just one moment ...

Mattie was laid to rest beside her mama, sister, and Orange under the 'ole oak tree.

Our hearts were broken as we all stood before the grave and wept until the tears would not flow anymore. An array of flowers was the last gift I could give to my dear Mattie. John Jack and me made a beautiful cross for Mattie's grave with her name on it. We put on it "Beloved mother, daughter, and sister." After the service, everyone went back to the house for supper and stories.

Yet I could not move. After some time had passed, John Jack came out to me and put a quilt around my shoulders, urging me to come inside.

I wanted to tell him how I could not leave Mattie all alone. My mind wandered back to the day when Mattie took me into her arms and welcomed me into her home. She never left me. Even when times were hard, she was always there. She was the one person I knew would never abandon me.

But I could not say these words because I could not speak.

I stood at Mattie's grave that day until darkness fell upon the mountain. The night cold crept into my body and chilled me to the bone. At some point, John Jack come out and walked me back to the house. I was put to bed by Mama and slept dream-free all night long. I stayed in bed the next day but was still unable to utter a single word. Mama worried and sent John Jack to see to me.

When John Jack arrived, I wanted to tell him how much I loved him, but I still could not speak. My world had collapsed and I had nothing to say.

John Jack then sent for Doc Austin, and after giving me a check-up he told Mama and John Jack I was in deep grief. "Nothing but time will do to heal her broken heart," he said.

I surely wasn't used to taking to bed, and although I hated everyone fussing on me, I was powerless to stop it. After some time, my mind cleared a bit. I remembered the dream I had the night before John Jack's wedding. *The whispers in the wind . . .*

The warning I could not hear then, but I heard now.

All the while I lay in bed sorting through my grief, Mama had sent for her things. She could not bear to leave me, and in fact, would never leave me again.

It took some time before I was back from my grieving. I reckoned my heart just needed to heal itself when it was good and ready. The morning I finally came down for breakfast, I found Mama in the kitchen.

She looked at me and smiled and said, "Good to have you back, Child."

It felt good to be among the living again. It was then I found out that Mama was staying, and I couldn't have been happier.

I uttered my first words in weeks and said, "Mama, I love you. I don't want today to pass without you knowing that."

Mattie left everything she owned to John Jack and me. The house and land was left in my name while her money was to be split evenly between the two of us. In a separate tin, she left a treasure map that her pappy made years ago. It showed an X on the map where he had supposedly buried his treasure.

Mattie left me a note that said:

My dearest Child,

I found this map in the shed many years ago after my pappy never came home that fateful winter. My mammy always said his mining for gold was pure nonsense, but I ain't so sure. I always wanted to believe in his stories, and I reckon that's why I never went looking for the treasure. It would have broke my heart to learn it might not be true.

Good luck finding the treasure, and I hope it's all that I ever dreamed it would be.

Love forever,
Mattie

I have never gone looking for that treasure. Since it meant so much to Mattie, it would have broke my heart too if I had found out it wasn't true. Dreams weren't meant to be broken ...

Mama had settled in nicely living back on the mountain and even went into town with me for supplies. The day we walked into the general store was something I will never forget. The local town folk whispered, as we were stirring up their day in a way that they could only dream of. Mama smiled ever so politely and went on about her business as if she had lived there all along. I guess in some strange way she never left. More importantly, Mama held her head high as she knew she had nothing to be ashamed about.

From that day on, things were different between the town folk and Mama. No more whispers were heard behind our backs. There were no more sly glances as we walked by or dirty looks from the older folk. I reckoned some things just ran their course, and most of the older town folk probably couldn't even remember why they had those feelings anyhow. Times were a changing, and it all felt right.

THE NEXT GENERATION

John Jack and Pearl had their first little boy a year after Mattie had passed. They named him Jackson, after John Jack, and he was the spitting image of his papa. Soon after, he was a big brother to August, who took after his mama. His blond hair and green eyes were a striking contrast to Jackson's dark hair and brown eyes, but needless to say, both boys took our breath away.

Mama and me spent many a day playing and teaching the boys about the mountain, just as Mattie and Orange had done for me and John Jack so very long ago.

Before long Pearl was pregnant again and blessed the family with a precious little girl. Mattie Rose was stunning and had features from both her mama and papa. Born with dark locks of curly hair and large green eyes, she seemed to have both of her folks' best features. She stole our heart the minute we set eyes on her. Our lives were forever changed for the better, and the mountain came alive with little ones living there again.

Sadly, not long after Mattie Rose had been born, on a beautiful spring day, Mama passed away. It was as if with one stroke of her paintbrush, she was gone. No storms raged or winds blew; in fact, the mountain was calm that day and I had no sense that anything was wrong. I found Mama slumped over in her rocking chair on the front porch with her sketchbook still in her lap. I like to think that she lived her last moment doing what she loved, living her dream.

Thankfully, Mama's last years were filled with much joy, more than she had ever expected or felt that she deserved. I guess you could say we had all come full circle. The mountain had called us all home; or maybe it was Mattie, working her magic by bringing everyone together one last time. Either way, we were a family, and nothing or nobody could change that.

So, here I sit in the same house I was reared in, under the same stars I have seen my entire life, and not for one minute did I wish I was anywhere else. To this day, when the wind snakes through the trees, I take pause and listen. Many a night, when the moon is showing off, I sit back and think about my years growing up on the mountain. I realize now how poor we had been all those years … poor only in the monetary sense, though, because in every other way, we was the richest folks around. By the time we actually had a little money, it didn't matter. We had each other, and that was worth far more than any goods money could buy.

I learned a lot from Mattie over the years, and one thing that still rings true to this day is that wishing is for the weak, but dreams are not. Dreams are meant to be lived. Sometimes I shined brighter than other times, but through it all, just like the firefly, I kept flying. Although I never fully recovered from the loss of Orange, Mattie, and Mama, I never really expected to either. Some love is just too deep to ever forget, and over the years I just learned how to live with the grief. Yet, even with the losses, I felt I had been blessed, truly blessed to live the years I did with my family on the mountain.

EPILOGUE

It seemed like I had talked for hours, and I reckoned I had. I looked out the window and saw a thin veil of darkness engulfing the mountain. My voice was hoarse, and I felt like I had been transported back in time. My mind felt heavy and foggy, like I had one foot in the past and one in the present.

I looked at my family as I tried to bring myself back from the life that seemed so long ago. Their eyes were moist with tears as they thanked me for sharing my memories.

Lightning crackled overhead, jolting me back and off in the distance, I heard a telephone ring.

"Papa says he is on his way," said Jackson.

"My dear brother ... Tell him not to hurry. The road up the mountain will be slick."

"Sure Auntie, sure."

I thought it was best if I did not tell the children about the dream I had last night. They might not understand, but I did. The storm tonight was for me, and I was not afraid. Still holding my beautiful emerald in my hands, I rubbed it one last time before putting it away in my wood box.

Oh, the emerald dreams ...

Leaning back in my chair, I closed my eyes and listened to the wind. Off in the distance I heard a lone wolf howl, and I felt strangely comforted.

The children's voices started to fade away and I felt myself weakening. I decided not to fight it; after all, this moment had been planned since the day I was born.

Outside the storm raged as I closed my eyes.

And I kept flying ...